EXACTING CLAM No. 7 — Winter 2022

CONTENTS

Front cover: "Claus Clams Up" by Walter Smart

Interior drawings by John Patrick Higgins, Kathleen Nicholls & Walter Smart

© 2022 Sagging Meniscus Press
All Rights Reserved

ISBN: 978-1-952386-52-7

Exacting Clam is a quarterly publication from Sagging Meniscus.

Senior Editors: Aaron Anstett, Jesi Bender, Jeff Chon, Elizabeth Cooperman, Tyler C. Gore, Charles Holdefer, Kurt Luchs, M.J. Nicholls, Doug Nufer, Thomas Walton

Executive Editor: Guillermo Stitch

Publisher: Jacob Smullyan

exactingclam.com

Kevin Boniface

HM Queen Elizabeth Has Died

September 9th 2022, 6.30am.
I switch on the ignition, the dashboard flickers and solemn radio voices in received pronunciation break the silence.

"As far as I have heard, within the next ten days or so, the Queen's body will be brought to London either by train or by air."

Twisting to fasten my seatbelt, I try to ignore the twinge in my lower back as I pull the van away from the kerb. I pass my neighbour, up early as usual walking his black Labrador. I skirt around the park where I wave to the woman with the Border terrier I always see there. On Fitzwilliam Street, the driver of the Star coaches bus has pulled into the lay-by for his regular cigarette.

In St Peter's Street I find the entrance to the yard blocked by two long-wheelbase Mercedes vans belonging to a hydraulic repair specialist. I park in the street and make my way over on foot.

On the loading bay, a group of men in mucky hi-vis are gathered around the buckled tail lift of one the 600s—the small seven and a half tonne trucks used on local dispatch—the cardboard insert from a roll container has been repurposed to soak up a large pool of oil under their feet.

I pass Brian in the stairwell, he's wearing a black armband.

"Where d'you get that?" I ask.

"It's a sock, Kev. I just cut the toe off."

I push through the scarred blue double doors onto the first floor where the radio is playing a succession of heartfelt ballads.

"I'm struggling a bit this morning, Kev" says Jimmy.

"Because of the Queen?" I ask.

"No, because I can't stand Celine Dion."

I dump my bag on my frame and adjust my knee support bandages.

Susan marches in: face mask, shorts, knee support bandages. She dumps her backpack on her frame.

"Hey, guess what? T'bloody 600's broke down!"

"I know" I say.

Two managers walk down the alley in shirts and ties and serious conversation; some football referee or other has had a right shocker. Lewis Capaldi's Hold Me While You Wait floods the shop floor while Susan explains that she's never considered herself much of a Royalist but last night she found herself in floods of tears. She's welling up now, while she's telling me. She says her and Douglas have a friend who's a taxi driver in Edinburgh and all the black cabs there have been lining the streets as a mark of respect. She reckons we should do something like that here.

"We should all get in us vans and drive round town in a big concave" she says.

She pulls a tissue from her sleeve and dabs at her eyes.

"I wish they hadn't called off the strike though" she says, "Me and Douglas were supposed to be going to Mathewson's in Thornton-Le-Dale today. You know? The place they film Bangers and Cash."

Adam arrives: bleached blond hair, shorts, knee support bandages. He dumps his bag on his frame.

"Bloody 600's broke down" he says.

"I know" say me and Susan.

He pulls a flask from his bag and takes a swig.

"How're you doing?" I ask.

He wipes his mouth with the back of his hand.

"I wasn't doing so bad until I came in here and had to listen to Jennifer Rush" he says, nodding towards the radio.

Adam thinks the union have let us down.

"They should have suspended the picket line but they shouldn't have abandoned the strike. What message does that send out? We look like a right pushover."

Simply Red's version of If You Don't Know Me By Now plays as Jimmy walks past with a handful of missorts.

"Bloody 600's broke down" he says.

"I know" say me, Susan and Adam.

We begin prepping our walks, sliding the mail into the slots on the frame. It's not as busy as we anticipated, perhaps the strike was called off too late for the night shift.

"Oh, I love this one though" say Adam and Susan when Endless Love by Diana Ross and Lionel Richie comes on.

Jimmy disagrees,

"It's horrible" he insists.

Out on delivery, the couch grass on the verges down to Spring Farm has been flattened in the heavy overnight rain and I find my usual parking spot occupied by a noisy electricity generator.

"T'bloody storm's brought all t'cables down, ha'n't it." explains Mr Boothroyd.

Mrs Sykes opens the door of the Lodge in the grounds of the Victorian mansion, she's in her dressing gown and tattoos.

"Good morning, love" she says and she takes her parcel.

The birch trees are shedding first this year; the track down to the stables is lined with a porridge of leaves.

I walk through a spider's web to give Mr Brooke his mail.

Nearly an hour in and no mention of the Royal News.

As I pass the window cleaner on the new estate of Executive Homes, he looks down from his ladder.

"Y'a'right, mate?" he says, as usual as I trip the noisy sonic deterrent that's designed to stop cats shitting on the plastic lawns. The skies brighten but in the lee of the cardboard box factory the road is still wet.

Mrs Mitchell tells me I'll not be calling as often now her son's gone off to university.

"He's the one who orders all the parcels" she explains.

At the old mill, the joiner with the tattooed calves has lost his van keys. His shouting Paul, another joiner with tattooed calves to see whether *he* knows where they are.

The two grey haired women in purple fleece jackets are walking down Old Moll Road as usual.

Mr Walker at Wrigley Court apologises for taking so long to get to his door. I explain I need to take a photograph of him holding the parcel and he calls his dog over so she can be in the picture too.

The man who always answers his door in the same dirty black t-shirt says exactly what he always says:

"Good morning. Thank you. Goodbye."

No mention of the Royal News. No mention of the fact that I'm supposed to be on strike.

I stop to empty the post box on Lea Lane, there's a single letter inside and the stamp has been eaten by the snails. This isn't the first time this has happened, they often nibble the envelopes and they seem to have a real taste for stamps in particular.

The woman from Cocking Steps passes with me her beagle where she always does, on the bridge. She gives me a wave and a cheery Hiya!

Two hours in and Mrs Hall is the first person to mention both the Royal News and the strikes. She's worried that the joint birthday party she's planned with her daughter will have to be cancelled because it falls during the official period of National Mourning. When she asks about the strike I tell her how we've all been standing about on the picket line drinking coffee.

"Wait there!" she says, and she disappears inside briefly before returning with a tin of Café de Panama from Fortnum & Mason, "Take this, it's gorgeous."

Mr Wilson on Lightenfield Lane has replaced the plastic container with the cracked lid he's used as a mail box since the early 2000s. His new box is of a very similar design but is obviously less weatherbeaten. When I open it I'm slightly disappointed to find that the faded 2004 copy of the Daily Mirror, which served as a lining and featured a picture Gary Neville lifting the FA Cup, has also been replaced. Folded into the bottom of the new box is a copy last week's Metro and a picture of Liz Truss.

I think about using the pair of buzzards that circle ominously above the idyllic rolling valley as an analogy for the sense of impending disaster enveloping the nation, but I decide not to bother.

At the building site which will soon be another new estate of Executive Homes, the call of the tiny blue nuthatch, thirty feet up in the sycamore, is easily loud enough to be heard above the cement mixers and JCBs. I think about somehow weaving a message of hope for the future around this little bird but it's hard to motivate myself.

On Midway I'm caught in a torrential downpour. A curtain of water sweeps across the valley, turning the streets into rivers and cleansing them of all the horse shit, dead wood and takeaway litter. I think about maybe putting together some kind of vengeful metaphor, but I decide there's not much point.

Number one Church Lane: "Thank you, bye bye."

Number sixteen: "Cheers! Bye bye now."

Number fifty-one: "Brilliant! Thanks, lad."

Five hours in and I call at Red Irene's with a parcel.

"What the hell do you think you're doing?" she says, "Why aren't you on strike?"

I explain that the strike has been put on hold because of the Royal News.

"Everything's been put on fucking hold!" she says. She takes the parcel and tells me to get myself back into the van and out of the rain.

I set off back to the office, past the dilapidated airfield where the engineering tycoons used to fly

in from Monte Carlo in the 1960s, past the derelict Standard Fireworks factory, past the rot-ting textile mills in the valley bottom, past the advertising hoarding on Manchester Road which is now hosting a memorial to the Queen, and past the long queue of people, mainly pensioners who are clutching bags for life. There are dozens of them lined up along the pavement outside the food bank, past the closed down pub and almost up to the pissy phone box where the man in the long overcoat used to go to read his Dean Koontz novels when it rained.

Back at the office I hand in my PDA at the key desk and report the snails in the post box to Stewart.

"Bloody molluscs" he says, "they've got no respect."

Paolo Pergola

Hurricanes, Typhoons and Cyclones

Fortunately, these natural phenomena do not usually occur in Italy, where I live. At the very most, we get a little gusty wind. Apparently, hurricanes, typhoons and cyclones are basically one and the same. What they are called depends on the geographical area where they go through. In Japan they're typhoons, I know that because I am visiting Japan and I just dodged one, typhoon number 12, called Jondari. I asked a Japanese friend of mine—Yuuki, I said, are these typhoons worse than hurricanes? and he answered, Nope, it's the same thing. And what about cyclones? Same thing. I was a little bit ashamed, I have to say, I guess we lack this cyclonic culture here in Italy.

If I understand correctly, then, hurricanes and typhoons are just like orcas and killer whales, or tungsten and wolfram. Same thing. In all cases they are a vortex of low pressure that rotates on itself and is formed near the equator due to the overheating of the ocean and so on and so forth. In the US they are called hurricanes, in the North Pacific they are called typhoons and in the South Pacific cyclones. But what if a hurricane, after hitting the US, decides to go to the left, that is to the east when looking at the map? It could reach Japan and then it should become a typhoon. That would be very confusing.

Not to mention their names; apparently, usually hurricanes are female. Well, not anymore, male names were added several years ago. I don't know if this is because the number of hurricanes has increased, or because there are more women meteorologists. Anyways, what they forgot to do, in Italian, is to match the gender to everything else. What's the point, for example, of calling a hurricane "Katrina"? It should be "Hurricaness Katrina". This thing of giving hurricanes people's names doesn't make that much sense. Hurricanes are bad news, see for example Katrina that wiped out New Orleans a few years ago. When you think "Katrina", you picture a beautiful girl, maybe Russian or Moldovan, perhaps a tennis player, let's say Katrina Makarova, a beautiful girl with a beautiful tennis-type body. Instead what you get is a hurricane that blows you away.

Apparently, it's not like when a hurricane shows up, people who run the hurricane business call someone with a degree in literature, and ask them, Hey, there is a hurricane coming, what should we call it? And the literature graduate, with all their literary culture, says, I think we should call it Katrina, because it reminds them of some literary characters from Chekhov or Gogol. Nope, it doesn't work like that. Apparently, the lists of names are all ready to go. And whoever came up with them must surely be someone with a degree in literature, but now that the lists are done, they were given the boot. We no longer need a literature graduate for the job, a hurricane shows up and we already know what to call it.

If I remember well, it's in alphabetical order, alternating female and male names. For example, in 2019 in the US the list started with Andrea, then Barry, Chantal, etcetera. Andrea is a girl's name in the US, however here in Italy it's a boy's name. That's quite confusing, not to mention that if a hurricane becomes a typhoon because it goes to Japan for a spin, the result would be some sort of gender-fluid, climatic-fluid phenomenon.

In addition, it seems that after a certain number of years, they restart from the beginning of the list. I believe it's after six or seven years. But every now and again, as it turns out, some names are removed from the list. For example, Katrina. Great. First you call this terrible hurricane with the name of a beautiful Russian tennis player from one of Gogol's novels, then you realize the mess you've made so you remove it? Isn't it a bit too late to change your mind? What about all the poor Russian girls named Katrina? Maybe there is one whose family lives in New Orleans because they immigrated, what should she do? Go to the town hall and change her name, just because of the literature graduate who wrote the list for which they were hired for a fixed term? If you really have to give hurricanes a person's name (though I don't understand why, other than it being the brilliant idea of some literature graduate), at least call them something else, something more appropriate, for example Attila, Adolf, Nero or Napoleon, things like that.

Melissa McCarthy

Liquid Systems

Through 2022 I was a roving, sometimes raving, reporter for a weekly online salon organized by the writer David Collard. Authors and artists from around the world, including many Exacting Clam *alumni and affiliates, would present and discuss their work there at the Glue Factory, and the Clam editors have kindly offered to disseminate a selection of my reports. Here's one from March, on cars, sharks, cyborgs and systems.*

Hello all.

I thought I would use this evening's talk to bring us up to date with everything that has been going on in the world of shark attacks.

I've got to disclaim at this point that, although I wrote a book with "Sharks" prominently in the title, I'm not actually interested in sharks. Not in-and-of themselves. I'm interested, rather, in what other areas sharks help me to think about; things like, "Death" or "Surfers." I use sharks, like a shark fisherman does, or much like Melville uses the body and the world of the whale, to discuss matters beyond just the sea creature. Although once you start looking, the body of the shark is actually fascinating, so maybe I can see why people become shark nerds, at that.

And as a writer, I'm interested, too, in how other people write about and imagine encounters with sharks. It's not so much the fact that occasionally in the water people intersect with sharks; this will obviously happen, sometimes. It's just one of those things. What I do look at is how these times and meetings are translated into text, what words and literature we craft out of the shark attack. And what else is included in the scenario, what else swims into view when a writer is describing a shark.

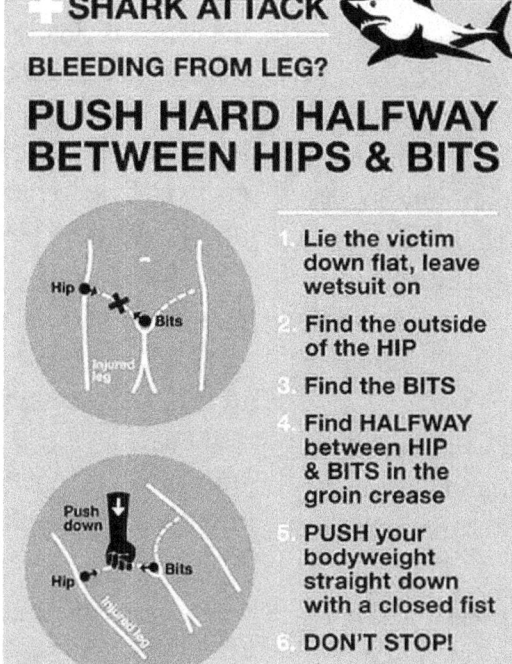

That's what I'll round up here: how human encounters with sharks are written about. It's a long story, but for this evening, I'll start about a hundred years ago and come swiftly up to date.

In 1916, there were the famous East Coast attacks, when several young men were killed in New Jersey, at first on the seaboard. But then the sharks started to come inland: into the bay, up the creeks, to the country villages, getting the farm boys. I learnt about this spate of attacks from the excellent *Shadows in the Sea*, by McCormick, Allen and Young.

This 1963 book demonstrates one of the things I look at in shark literature, which is, its binocular (and more) aspect: a work tells us about the time that it's describing, but also of course about the time that it's written. Then the third, extending or perhaps triangulating aspect is the time of our reading. In this book, the authors in 1963 high-

light that this 1916 "shark season" coincided both with American entry into World War 1 and with an epidemic of polio. In the early sixties, these are the aspects that the authors picked out, about events of fifty years earlier.

I was much taken by their noticing of polio, a disease that gets into the blood system then lurks there, circulating, waiting for the time to pounce. There's a lot to be investigated in this contrast between the paralysis of polio, the immobility it causes, versus its then-mysterious spread, its fluidity (there was a strong fear that you could catch it in swimming pools, from the water). Then there's a third strand, with the development of inoculation, distributing the vaccine. I think there's an interesting parallel between polio and the shark, with its stillness, its speed, its hiddenness.

The 1916 attacks return as a concern of Brody and Hooper in the 1975 film (not the book) of *Jaws*. You see them babbling on to the mayor:

> "It's gonna happen again, it's happened before, the Jersey beach, right—nineteen sixteen—there were five people—five people—they were chewed up in the surf—in one week."

This—*Jaws*—is another manifestation of shark attack.

Now I'll circle back to 1958, and the establishment of the International Shark Attack File, an initiative in which one of my elasmobranch heroes, Dr. Samuel Gruber, was heavily involved. The File is a proper academically-maintained database of shark attack events, which offers an excellent questionnaire for participants to fill in.

Sample questions: please describe the type, number, size of your assailant. With the great instruction: use extra pages if necessary.

Next shark encounter: Lew Boren, surfer, killed by a great white shark off the California coast in 1981, as described in Kief Hillsbery's excellent article in issue 375 of *Rolling Stone* magazine. A vital point about Lew Boren's death is what it gives the journalist an opportunity to talk about, which is, society and its changes. He uses the life and death of Lew Boren as a microcosm of or parable for the incipient Reagan era: "Lew was amazing: a 60s person in an 80s world." But Lew does not survive.

Next: 2014, Australian attack, swimmer killed, only her little red bathing cap found, floating on the surface. It's the details that grab the reader, in the story.

September 2021: I read an article that is not a report of an attack, but a description of a new technique for stopping blood loss, devised by Dr Nicholas Taylor, associate dean of the Australian National University, and a surfer. Published in the *Journal of Emergency Medicine Australasia* in February, his idea is to help people who have been bitten by a shark. If there's damage to the femoral artery, which can cause a lot of trouble, rather than tangling around with a tourniquet, the new technique is to exert firm pressure down on the mid hip-crease using a rigid arm. And there's a slogan to help remember this, which is, "Push hard halfway between hips and bits."

The article I read described this as a mnemonic, which I'm not sure that it is; it's just a phrase. But I'll come back to this idea, to Taylor's medical technique, at the end.

February 2022: recent, sad death of a British swimmer in Australia: the witness recounts that the attacking shark "looked like a car in the water."

This is a vital point: sharks as vehicles. I'm always going on about this: that cars are sharks.

Why? Because they are sleek, long, dark vehicles that go fast. With fins. Because when there is a collision between a car / shark and a person, it's usually detrimental to the person. The shark and the car, particularly in dramatic situations, can contain people whose encounter with it has proved fatal. Also, as I suggested at the start, sharks and cars too are vehicles for meaning: they are *metaphores*, removal vans, for shifting meanings about to new places.

I'll bring in here the French author Roland Barthes and his book *Mythologies*, a collection of essays written between 1954 and 1956, published in 1957. The first English translation was in 1972, and I have a Vintage Classics edition from 2000, translated by Annette Lavers, which has a back cover blurb from playwright Dennis Potter that reads:

> Semiology is the study of the signs and signals, the symbols, gestures and messages through which western society sustains, sells, identifies and yet obscures itself by painting or powdering over its raddled, whore-like visage . . .

Which I fear tells us a lot more about Dennis Potter than it does about French philosophy. But in relation to Barthes, I'd like to discuss probably the most famous essay in *Mythologies*, which is about a type of car, the Citroën D.S. 19. I'll just recap the basics, for anyone who is uninterested in cars, or not familiar with this utterly beautiful one, produced between 1955 and 1975 (the year I was born).

The initials in the name are just letters, as far as I know, not code for anything automotive. But pronounced in French as D S (day, ess), they sound the same as déesse, the word for goddess. There's also a cheaper model, same body but less powerful, called the I D (ee, day), like the word idée, which means idea. Calling your lovely new vehicles Goddess and Idea is quite something, especially as the long-running previous main model from Citroën was the more pedestrian

Traction Avant, which has completely different linguistic connotations. And, the Traction just looks like a car from a previous century; they are comically different.

With the D.S., the normal shape is swooping down from front to back, like pompadoured hair. But there's also a station wagon version, so that you can put your surfboards in the back or on top; an ambulance version that a stretcher fits in; the snazzy D super 5; and the Pallas, after the Greek goddess Athena, which opens up a whole new vista of mythology.

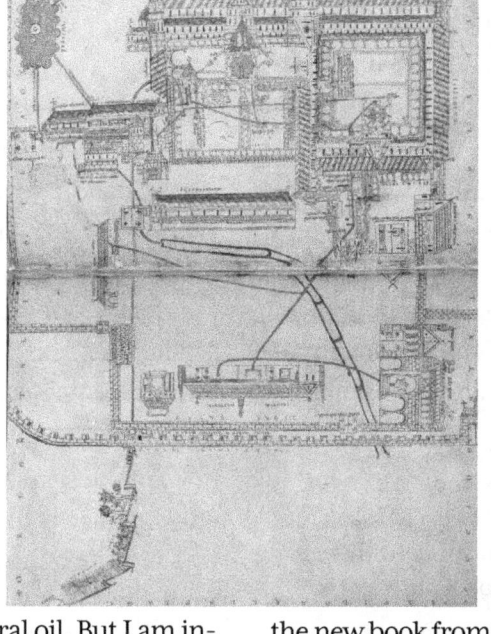

There are plenty of design innovations in the D.S., but one of the most notable is that is has hydro-pneumatic suspension throughout, instead of metal springs, which gives some technical blah about control, handling, as well as comfort. I'm not so interested in that as in the fact that it's liquid throughout the system. Not water, but a mineral oil. But I am interested in all watery systems. In flow, motion, vehicles.

Anyway, lovely car, a liquid system, vocabulary that expands out in new directions: all this is good. What Barthes says about the D.S. is quite famous. He opens:

The New Citroën

I think that cars today are almost the exact equivalent of the great Gothic cathedrals: I mean the supreme creation of an era, conceived with passion by unknown artists, and consumed in image if not in usage by a whole population which appropriates them as a purely magical object.

The car's smoothness, he says, reveals perfection, the beyond human, just like Christ's robes, or sci-fi airships. And he talks of

A new phenomenology of assembling, as if one progressed from a world where elements are welded to a world where they are juxtaposed and hold together by sole virtue of their wondrous shape.

The whole short essay is lovely, it's quicker to read it yourself than for me to paraphrase, but details include Barthes saying that the D.S.'s glass is beautiful, like soap-bubbles or "a substance more entomological than mineral," and that the car is engaged in moving categories, from the engine to the organism.

And he talks about the tactile pleasure of the design: "one pretends to drive with one's whole body." It's an almost *Crash*-like merging of the human body, with the beetle, with the metal, with the mineral: an unbroken, a smooth combining of materials into a new schema. (I'm looking forwards to reading the new book from Harry Parker, my fellow guest this evening: *Hybrid Humans*, about how we design and merge with our machinery.)

So, there's a particular car as described by Barthes in pre-1957, in the fun, first half of his *Mythologies*. In the second half of the book, he expounds on the function of myth as a type of language within society, and the political ramifications of this. This section is much denser, but it does contain this simile, near the end: "Just as the cuttlefish squirts its ink in order to protect itself, it [bourgeois ideology] cannot rest until it has obscured the ceaseless making of the world, fixated this world into an object which can be for ever possessed," etc.

Even Barthes in full revolutionary spate comes back to talking about, using the metaphor of, a sea-creature on the attack. He's a shark reporter, too.

As a side observation, what I get from reading his report on cars from so long ago, is that observation does not become dated: if you keep your eyes peeled, look at the world carefully, it's never not important; it's Ezra Pound's "News that stays news." Barthes was looking at the D.S., and that's what I do too. I'm just part of a tradition, a long school or shoal of observers, who notice shark incidents and write about them. I'm looking at the cars, thinking about the sharks and the language.

Before I close I want to come back to the 2021 report of a new method for dealing with bleeding, the "push halfway" mantra. It's a suggestion that's been highly commended by other emergency medicine specialists. Dr. Anthony Brown, fish boffin and professor at the University of Queensland, says that it's brilliant, "a fantastic life-saving idea." He goes on:

> Your sole priority needs to be to stop the bleeding and wait for help. You're a bit buggered if you're the only one there, but generally speaking there is someone else there to help. Nobody surfs alone.

This is nice. It might not be factually correct, but as a statement of intent, a principle, it's great. Nobody surfs alone. This is what I want to end on. Barthes is from nearly seventy years ago, but his attention to detail never gets old. This is what keeping abreast of shark attack news, with its intricate entanglement with cars, has taught me, that I'd like to report to you: That there are always more details in the language, and, nobody surfs alone. It's a message of solidarity.

Thanks.

KURT LUCHS

AREA SATIRE RAG TURNS 35

THE REAL HISTORY OF FAKE NEWS AND THE CULTURAL ROLE OF HUMOR IN OUR TIME

Do you recall reading such news stories as these: "Drugs Win Drug War," "'I May Be Hazardous To Your Health,' Warns Homicidal Surgeon General," "Allstate Charged With Operating Protection Racket," "ACLU Defends Nazis' Right To Burn Down ACLU Headquarters," "Congress Passes Americans With No Abilities Act," or "America Online To Build Three Million Home Pages For The Homeless"?

If you recognize any of these funny headlines, or even the style of them, then you're undoubtedly familiar with the *Onion*, at one time America's favorite online source of fake news—at least until the last two presidential elections. If so, you're also familiar with my work, because I wrote those headlines and some of the accompanying stories, and hundreds more.

Yet for a publication that celebrates its 35th birthday this year (2023), and achieved notoriety ever since the internet took off in the mid-nineties, little is known about the real history of the *Onion* and where it fits into the pop culture continuum. Even less is known about the inner workings of the *Onion*'s special approach to humor. Who puts it together, and how do they do that week after week?

Well, today, as the saying goes, we're going to unscrew the inscrutable. We'll peel back the layers of the *Onion* to see where it came from, and where it fits in the history of America's written humor, flowing naturally out of literary traditions begun by the *New Yorker*, the *National Lampoon* and *Saturday Night Live*. Using my 10 simple rules for funny headlines, we'll learn how to create funny fake news the *Onion* way, which we'll see is a serious discipline that can teach us how to think creatively and concisely, whether as humor writers or as journalists—assuming there's still a difference. And we'll examine some of the implications, both positive and negative, of a comedic world where fake news increasingly reigns.

Though hundreds of articles and news reports have been done about the *Onion*, certain key facts of its true history have never been told—how the paper really got its name, for instance. Scott Dikkers, the founding editor who made the *Onion* what it is, sometimes tells reporters that "onion" is an old slang term for a juicy news story. Baloney! The *Onion* started in 1988 in Madison, Wisconsin as an unofficial response to the official University of Wisconsin school paper the Union. So the *Onion* name is just a pun, and not a very sophisticated one, which is no doubt why they try to keep the truth a secret.

For its first year it wasn't even a funny paper, merely a run-of-the-mill alternative paper. Under Dikkers' leadership in 1989 they started making serious fun of the university and the town, and that purely local humor was their stock-in-trade for five years until 1994, when their content became national in focus.

When the internet began to transform the world around 1995, the *Onion* was one of the first publications to go online. It was a happy accident, not clever strategy, that they were the first high-quality humor outlet to bring unique content to the web, and that, coupled with their new national focus, made them famous almost overnight. I started writing for them the following year, and was the only non-staff writer contracted to work on their first book "Our Dumb Century" three years later in 1999.

That book went on to win the country's highest literary humor award, the Thurber Prize.

Though its moment in the sun has arguably passed, today the *Onion* is still one of the most popular and critically acclaimed humor publications in the world, with millions of hits on its web site every week, and a string of best-selling books.

It's worth noting, however, that while the *Onion* has perfected the modern fake news format, they did not invent it. That honor goes to the National Lampoon magazine, which started its News On the March feature in 1970, as was pointed out to me personally by one of the original Lampoon writers and editors, my friend and mentor the late George Trow. When painter Pablo Picasso died, News On the March announced, "Picasso Enters Black Period." With its concision, its irony and its sense of the macabre, that could easily be an *Onion* headline. And in fact the parallels between the history of the National Lampoon and the history of the *Onion* run much deeper than that, as we shall see.

But I don't want to get ahead of myself. One of the things I want to bring out here is the idea that the success of the *Onion* is not unprecedented. This has happened before in our country. Several times, in fact.

So let's pause right here for a brief—well, not too brief—parenthesis about the history of written humor in America. From the founding of the nation up through the nineteenth century, the pickings are pretty slim and that history can be summarized with two names: Mark Twain and Ambrose Bierce. One might also mention Supreme Court Justice Oliver Wendell Holmes and his lone contribution to humor, a charmingly gentle book called "The Autocrat of the Breakfast Table." Look it up; it's well worth checking out.

The key point about Twain and Bierce is that, while their work is often animated by topical concerns, it almost always transcends them. The laughter comes mainly from absurdities of human nature and the human condition that are perennial. This puts them in a straight line of descent from Chaucer and Shakespeare. And this is why their work lives today and the work of all of their contemporaries is as dead as the age of silent movies.

The first half of the twentieth century was a golden age for written humor, highlighted by the founding of the *New Yorker* in 1925. Note the date: right smack in the middle of the Roaring Twenties. Insofar as the *New Yorker* can be seen as a response to its time, it was a reaction to the decade of the "lost generation," those who had come back from World War One having fought the war to end all wars and returned home to find that, thanks to Prohibition, they were no longer legally allowed to enjoy the same beverages they had enjoyed while putting their lives on the line. There was a new social and sexual freedom, a new prosperity (for a while, anyway), and a new form of popular music, jazz, all lubricated by bootleg liquor provided by organized crime.

The *New Yorker* was not unique. There were a dozen or so national humor magazines with high literary standards at that time. Yes, Virginia—before the internet, before television, before radio, before universal public education, Americans actually knew how to read and write and laugh at things that did not insult their intelligence. The *New Yorker* simply happens to be the only such publication that has survived, and it did so precisely by becoming more than a humor magazine after the vogue for humor magazines had passed. Nearly every major metropolitan newspaper had at least one humor columnist, and many of those writers enjoyed national reputations that were well deserved.

The early *New Yorker* was much more humor-based than the magazine is today. Even their serious stuff had an amusing edge because their hu-morists wrote much of it. The young *New Yorker* gave us S.J. Perelman, who also co-wrote several early Marx Brothers films, as well as Dorothy Parker, Robert Benchley and James Thurber. For my money, Benchley is the best of that bunch, and arguably the finest American humorist of all time. But it was Thurber whom Ernest Hemingway described as "one of the least boring writers who ever lived." High praise indeed from Papa, who was not typically generous with compliments.

The *New Yorker* was and is a weekly magazine. Much of the humor that appeared there was topical, dealing with transient events of the day. The best of it, though—which I take to be most of the work by Benchley and Thurber—draws more upon human frailties and foibles and less on news or controversies of the moment. Hold that thought, because it will lead us back to the *Onion*.

Eventually the old guard of *New Yorker* humor writers died off or lost their edge. The second-string writers who replaced them—people like Peter DeVries—were frankly not of the same caliber. By the nineteen-sixties, the magazine had been transformed from a devil-may-care satirical outlet into a rather staid, if very well done, outlet for other kinds of literature and serious journalism. The best humor in the *New Yorker* was in the cartoons, as is still the case today.

Then two things happened. At the *New Yorker*, a second golden age of humorous prose slowly began. Woody Allen's first piece for them appeared in 1966, Garrison Keillor's in 1969. The nineteen-seventies brought comedic bylines from George Trow, Ian Frazier, and Veronica Geng, the funniest woman since Dorothy Parker. Together they ushered in a new sharpness, a new edge to written humor in this country. Since then, others such as Jack Handey and David Sedaris have continued that forward movement.

The second thing that happened along with the *New Yorker's* new golden age was that the success of the Harvard Lampoon, a university humor magazine that had achieved some national notoriety, led in 1970 to the creation of the National Lampoon, a humor magazine that was everything the *New Yorker* was not at that time: vulgar, profane, dark, and deeply cutting. Where the *New Yorker* would take the nation's pulse like a wise and trusted family physician, the National Lampoon always went straight for the jugular. I would be embarrassed to try to read aloud in mixed company from any of their more infamous articles. But just the title alone should tell you something about a story called "Children's Letters to the Gestapo."

Unlike the *New Yorker*, both the Lampoon and the *Onion* have their roots on campus. Each of them came along at a certain point in time and took written humor someplace it hadn't been before.

At the time the Lampoon started in 1970 the country was undergoing a kind of mass psychosis consisting of equal parts of Vietnam, the Baby Boom youth culture led by the Beatles, and the relatively new phenomenon of universal college education. All of these things led to the so-called "generation gap," a greater divide between generations than we have seen in this country before or since—until the last couple of years, that is. For the first time in the age of mass media there was a whole population of rebellious, educated young people looking for entertainment that spoke to them. The *New Yorker* had expressed the right opinions to suit that generation, it opposed the war and so on, yet it did not speak to them in their language.

The Lampoon was a more visceral response to a certain moment in time, and in particular to continuing the Vietnam War and the political establishment behind the war. It's significant that when Richard Nixon resigned in disgrace in 1974, and that establishment was seen as overthrown, the Lampoon's reason for being suddenly disap-

peared, and it began a swift decline. By 1980 it was creatively and financially dead, though it limped along in various lesser forms into the nineties. In its final days as an online publication it became a pale imitation of the *Onion*, which was some kind of poetic justice, or injustice.

Today, of course, the National Lampoon is known primarily as a god-awful movie franchise, which regularly spews out such abominations as "Van Wilder." In the beginning, however, it was a brilliant magazine. In less than five years after it began the Lampoon extended its franchise successfully into books, record albums, stage shows, and a radio series called "The National Lampoon Radio Hour," which was, characteristically, 30 minutes long. That's where Christopher Guest and the other "Spinal Tap" performers got their start. When the Lampoon did get into the movie business, their first features, "Animal House" and "National Lampoon's Vacation," were commercially and critically successful.

Oddly enough, the one nut they were never able to crack was television, and this is one more thing they have in common with the *Onion*. Another Lampoon alumnus is Tony Hendra (you may recognize him as band manager Ian Faith in the movie "Spinal Tap"). In his book "Going Too Far" Hendra describes how the Lampoon's cleverest writers defected from their employer precisely because of its failure to penetrate the world's most popular medium. They helped Lorne Michaels start *Saturday Night Live*, essentially creating the fake television news format when they turned the Lampoon's News On the March feature into Weekend Update.

More recently, in an ironic example of history repeating itself, writers like Ben Karlin and David Javerbaum left the *Onion* to take charge of *The Daily Show* and *The Colbert Report*. Just as *Saturday Night Live* was an unofficial spinoff of the *National Lampoon*, *The Daily Show* and *The Colbert Report* were unofficial spinoffs of the *Onion*. These are the TV shows the

Onion should have been doing if it could get its act together as a business. For the past decade or so the *Onion* has been trying to rectify this mistake by getting into the online viral video business. Thus, instead of conquering the old form of video entertainment, television, they may succeed through bypassing it altogether for a new form. They have experienced many ups and downs, and the jury is still out.

Having examined the *Onion*'s history and influences, let's look at what makes it unique. The *Onion* has cornered the market on a special brand of funny news. But how do they do it? How do they create this level of material week in and week out?

First let's mark the differences between fake news as it existed before the *Onion*, and after. *Saturday Night Live's Weekend Update* is always very specifically topical, its funny headlines reflecting exactly what was in the news that week. The *Onion* is often topical that way, and has become more topical in recent years due to competitive pressures from all directions, but it is still not topical as much or as often as you might think. Usually the *Onion* is more what I would call generically topical. They don't always base their fake news on a particular piece of real news. And when they do, it is more often to make some larger satirical point.

For instance, when tornadoes hit the Midwest one week, the *Onion* headline was, "Tornado Violence: Could It Be Caused By Tornadic Images In The Media?" That is flat-out brilliant satire, taking a real-life event—a tragedy, in fact—and turning it into a much broader comment on Hollywood, political correctness and sloppy reasoning. The coining of the fake, pompous-sounding word "tornadic" is particularly clever. That is something you will never see on any of the late-night shows. But how do you get there creatively?

When I started writing for the *Onion* I found it helpful to think through the process in depth, analyzing it and creating my own 10 rules for writing fake headlines the *Onion* way. I know my rules work, because in addition to using them myself I have mentored several young writers into becoming *Onion* contributors over the years.

Rule Number 1: The headline comes first. With real news, of course, the story is written first, then the headline. But we're making the news up, remember? Headlines like "Court Takes Custody Of Harley From Unfit Motorcycle Mama" are not based on actual events. Writing the headline first also helps test and perfect the comedic premise of the story. Which brings us to:

Rule Number 2: The whole joke must be present in the headline. Why? Because with fake news as with real news, some people only read headlines, and you want them to get the essence of the joke. Also, the *Onion* is a communal enterprise in which any headline can be assigned to any writer to complete the story. This is one reason they don't give bylines. One of the first *Onion* ideas I had rejected was called "Death Takes A Holiday." It was a story about Death needing a little time off to put up some paneling in his rec room. It was actually a fairly funny story, but it failed to make the cut because it didn't focus on the headline first. After I understood that, I was able to write headline jokes that were complete in themselves, such as "Mental Hospital Fire Leaves Hundreds Of Demons Homeless" and "134-Year-Old Man Attributes Longevity To Typographical Error."

Rule Number 3: Keep it short. A two-word funny headline that contains a complete joke is perhaps the hardest thing in the world to write (besides a large check). Twelve words is about the maximum for a good *Onion* headline, five or six words a good target. Subheads should be used sparingly because they can become a form of cheating. One of my bits in the book "Our Dumb Century" is on a front page dated February 4, 1932. Under the section entitled Business News is the simple headline "Apple Sold," which encapsulates in two words the business climate of the Great Depression, a climate we are probably on the verge of learning about all over again. A little later I did a brief news item entitled "Cricket Located." I have tried in vain, many times, to write a one-word headline joke. That feat continues to elude me.

Rule Number 4: Both quality and quantity count when generating funny ideas. The *Onion* staff discipline used to be to submit 25 headlines at each weekly meeting—a discipline I kept for many years. The group task of winnowing through the many hundreds or thousands of ideas submitted each week is ruthless. It consists of a quorum of the full-time editors and writers congregating in a conference room and pitching their own ideas along with many submitted by freelancers. That process is brutal. Total unanimity is not needed for an idea to succeed, but if even one person absolutely hates it, it generally gets thrown on the trash heap of history. There is an ebb and flow to the process, and one sometimes senses that the *Onion* writers have tired of an idea or a style before their audience has, which I suppose is a good thing. The *Onion* Editor-in-Chief used to keep a running index of about 5,000 headlines, which was constantly pruned. Many good ideas made that list only to fall off without being used. Only about 15 find their way into print each week. I don't know if they still maintain that master list. The competition is fierce and becomes more intense every year. So many headlines are submitted now that the weekly quota has been reduced from 25 to 15, giving writers like me even fewer chances to make it into the paper.

Rule Number 5: Use topical subjects mainly to get at larger issues. Again, this is not the approach of *Saturday Night Live* and *Weekend Update*. For instance, my headline "Gay Gene Isolated, Ostracized" is hopefully funny, yes, but the humor is also intended as a broader comment. Normally the word "rape" should never appear in a joke, but I tried to kill two birds with one stone when I wrote: "Raped Environment Led Polluters On, Defense Attorneys Argue." Hopefully the larger satirical purpose justifies the liberties taken. Very often this kind of satire can be aimed at our consumer culture, with stories like "Pantene Introduces New Behavioral Conditioner" and "Learning Channel Switches To All-Gilligan Format."

Rule Number 6: The *Onion*'s mainstays have always been a catchall category I call "pure goofiness, non sequiturs, and reductio ad absurdum." I think you know what goofiness is. It's headlines like the very first cover story I wrote for the paper, "Dalai Lama Decks Photographer In Disco Melee." Non sequitur is Latin for "It does not follow." Some examples would be "Vocalist Leaves Journey Tribute Band Over Creative Differences," "Supermodels Form Hall Of Justice To Protect Ordinary Models," and "Rubenesque Woman Has Picassoesque Face." Reductio ad absurdum is another bit of Latin, a fancy way of saying you're taking a premise to its logical (yet absurd) conclusion. You might start with the premise of Civil War reenactments and end up with the headline, "Civil War Enthusiasts Burn Atlanta To Ground." Or another one from "Our Dumb Century," "FDR's Remains To Run For Fifth Term."

Rule Number 7: Raise the trivial to the significant. In short, take something utterly unimportant and treat it like front-page news. I tried this with headlines like "Star Trek Introduces Character With Totally Different Forehead Wrinkles," "Nation's Substitute Teachers Would Like To Know Who Threw That," and "Birthday Boy Admits Accepting Gifts." Of course, raising the trivial to the significant is what made stars of those famously mundane *Onion* characters, Area Man and Area Woman. Every *Onion* contributor enjoys writing about those two. One of my efforts was "Nutrisystem Helps Area Man Lose $277."

Rule Number 8: Lower the significant to the trivial. This was my aim with such headlines as

"Nation's Educators Alarmed By Poorly Written Teen Suicide Notes" "Aching Void Filled By Profusion Of Goods," and "10th Circle Added To Rapidly Growing Hell." The latter took on a life of its own, getting transformed into the title of an *Onion* book, "Dispatches From The 10th Circle," and becoming the first and so far the only *Onion* story to be sold to Hollywood (I wrote the headline, Todd Hanson wrote the story). It was bought by DreamWorks to be made into an animated feature film. And no, I never saw a dime of that money. In fact, I never heard about the sale from the *Onion*. I read about it in the Chicago Tribune like everyone else. Still, I can say that Steven Spielberg bought something of mine. But I digress . . .

Rule Number 9: Report: Fake research can be howlingly funny. Adding a fake authority to fake news can notch up the laughter, as in headlines like "Report: Aspirin Taken Daily With Bottle Of Bourbon Reduces Awareness Of Heart Attacks," "Human Feet Originally Used For Walking, Anthropologists Report," and "Study: Nonconformity Linked To Peer Pressure."

Rule Number 10: Clever reiteration works. Did I mention that clever reiteration works? We don't know why—probably it has something to do with timing or rhythm, or something in our evolutionary history. But the humor of reiteration is what I was going for in these headlines: "New Starbucks Opens In Rest Room Of Existing Starbucks," "Department Of Health, Education And Welfare To Destroy Nation's Health, Education And Welfare," "Billy Joel Has Billy Joel's Disease," "AIDS Awareness Campaign Spreads Awareness, AIDS," "Test Tube Baby Reunited With Test Tube," "Man Prone To Lying Beds Woman Prone To Lying Prone," and my personal favorite, with three reiterations in just five words, "New Envelope Pushes Envelope Envelope." One of my colleagues then came up with another good reiteration joke: "Friend Of Friend Better Friend Than Friend." Seven words, with four repetitions of one word. He beat me! The gauntlet

has definitely been thrown. I tried and tried to come up with a topper for that one, but no luck.

So much for the 10 rules of writing for the *Onion*.

In the interest of journalistic integrity and full disclosure, I must admit that the overwhelming popularity of the *Onion*'s fake news format is not necessarily all good news. One potential danger of getting too much news "fortified with irony" is that it may cause a toxic level of cynicism about people and institutions—a comedy writer's occupational hazard, as I can personally attest.

I also worry that it may foster a lack of depth, an environment where all news becomes "infotainment," mere fodder for punch lines. There are signs that fake news may even have begun to overtake real news for some of us. A number of research reports have found that a significant percent of young people get their news from comedy shows like *Saturday Night Live* and *The Daily Show*. Should we be troubled by this? Or glad that at least our more laughter-loving young people are getting their news somewhere? It may be the comedy-writing cynic in me, but I can't help but wonder—are we more likely to self-destruct from cynicism . . . or naïveté?

Which leads me to another question that will occur to most religious believers (of which, I hasten to add, I am not one): Is nothing sacred? Is there anything a spiritually-minded comedy writer won't, on principle, make fun of? Or even a "spiritual but not religious" comedy writer like myself? For me, the short answer is: no.

Let me expand on that a bit. When the members of Monty Python sat down to write the script that became *Life of Brian*, they were originally going to call it *Jesus Christ—Lust for Glory*. Remember, though, these were Cambridge men, Oxford men. They knew how to do their homework. So to prepare themselves for the task they all read the Gospels. And a funny, unexpected thing happened. No, none of them were converted. But they quickly realized that, while they might not accept Jesus as God, just as I cannot, neither could they ridicule Him. He was too real for that. The Gospels were too sobering. So they came up with the idea of a reluctant false messiah, a man living a life parallel to Jesus, this man Brian who was mistaken for the Savior and crucified right along with Him. What a clever way to make fun of the various ways that humans misuse religion and yet still allow the humorists to maintain their newfound respect for Jesus.

The point of the story is: context. In comedy as in any other art, context matters.

All that said, when you see something downright sacrilegious in the *Onion* or the *Onion* books, it (probably) wasn't written by me. However, I do believe there is a way to find humor in almost anything. A silly example would be "Nation's Stray Dogs Call For Increased Wino-Vomit Production." Now that's just gross, scatological body function humor. But following the Amish comedy writing principle of only using words that can be found in the Bible, well, we do find wine and vomit and dogs in there, don't we? I did write one profane headline that they never used: "'Jesus Fucking Christ!' Prays Monk With Tourette's." No comment necessary.

A less silly example would be my story "God Answers Prayers Of Paralyzed Little Boy; 'No,' Says God." Admittedly, that is dark. So dark that the *Onion* later made it into a refrigerator magnet so that they could spread the joy! It makes you laugh and cringe at the same time, and it's meant to. But if you are a religious believer, it also happens to be theologically sound. And it tries to find a comedic outlet for some genuine human pain around the issues of free will, divine intervention, and a world where the principalities and powers still think they're calling the shots, and paralyzed little boys do in fact die with their prayers not answered the way we would wish.

Staying with the idea of context for a moment, what is the context for the *Onion* itself? If the *New Yorker* came out of the Roaring Twenties and the *National Lampoon* out of the rebellious sixties, what is the significance of the *Onion* coming to prominence in what might be called the Nothing Nineties? I mean, that was the Clinton decade. Was there a crying need to make fun of Clinton? This was a president about whom the average citizen could easily write their own punch lines.

I believe the context for the *Onion* was less political than social and technological. The *Onion* was the first original product to arise from and address the internet age. The context for the *Onion* is a nation swiftly leaving behind the hegemony of three major television networks, a time when new music still debuted on the radio, when movies could only be seen in theatres or in TV reruns, and when big city newspapers still dreamed they could tell people what to think. The world that has been emerging is one in which there are many media and a potentially infinite number of channels in each medium, including social media.

Make no mistake, no one is a bigger fan than I am of this world of ever-expanding, user-based media. I love freedom. I love having choices. But I would also argue that this world has tended to make us more focused on the transient moment. I call it "living in the narcissistic bubble of the now." Instead of the shared experience of our common humanity, which has been the source of the richest humor of the past, we share mainly the superficial recounting of mostly trivial events and nonevents. Humor and comedy have become almost exclusively topical and separated from the stream of history and genuine humanity. As we have seen, the *Onion* has found some clever ways around this problem by being generically topical. Yet it must be admitted that to some extent, the *Onion* and the revolution it helped usher in are also part of the problem.

And because of that, some of us in the humor writing business have begun to bite the hands that feed us. The *New Yorker* continues to publish some of the best humorous prose in the country, but it no longer leads the pack. The torch for the type of literary humor that is not in the *Onion* fake news mold has been passed to a group of half a dozen online literary humor magazines. The one that started it all is *McSweeney's Internet Tendency*, and the others, such as my own publication *The Big Jewel* (now defunct), were inspired by it. While the combined audience for these sites is nowhere near that of the *Onion*, their influence among humor writers and readers is extensive. Many of the best humor writers alive at the moment appear in these venues. It remains to be seen whether these small fish, swimming against what appears to be the tide of history, can make a difference.

Lately *McSweeney's Internet Tendency*, along with the *Onion* and the *New Yorker*, has become much more topical and political in the Trump era. While I understand the impulse and timing of it, I question whether this is the best move creatively or culturally, or even politically. Why should one substandard politician be allowed to suck up all the oxygen in the room? Wouldn't it be more of an actual victory to focus on other things, to show that life goes on? Which, in fact, it does. Nor is most of what matters in life about politics or ideology, which, in the end, are so hideously goddamned boring even to ridicule. (Here endeth the sermon.)

It is sad, comedically and creatively, that the great majority of online humor sites and late-night TV shows only lean left or even hard left. On the right or center-right in late night, there is only *Gutfeld*, and it doesn't surprise me that he is bigger than all the rest. In his niche he's running unopposed. On the right in online humor, there is only the *Babylon Bee*, to which the *Onion* seems to have unintentionally passed the torch, because the *Onion* has somewhat succumbed to wokeness and political one-sidedness. When President Biden announced that his Supreme Court nominee would be a Black woman, the *Babylon Bee's* headline was "Biden Seen Looking At Paint Color Swatches To Choose Next Supreme Court Justice." In bygone years that could have been an *Onion* story. No more.

I don't pretend to know the answers to all of these questions about the ascendancy of fake news as the uber-comedy of our time. But I do know that whatever its dangers, such comedy can also function as prophecy, truth-telling and a way to keep the powerful honest, if it doesn't pull its punches for political reasons, as the *Onion* has been doing since at least the 2016 election. I'm reminded of the infamous essay by Jonathan Swift, "A Modest Proposal." Swift used a savage satiric premise worthy of the *Onion*—cannibalism, of babies, no less—to expose England's oppression of the Irish. The *Onion's* first post-9/11 issue played a similar role in helping us deal with the terror attacks, with stories like "Hijackers Surprised To Find Selves In Hell" and "God Angrily Clarifies 'Don't Kill' Rule." Would that they recommitted to that kind of satiric relevance.

Finally, I have discovered an unexpected of benefit of learning how to write fake headlines: It sharpened my ability to interpret and judge real ones. You see, once you become an expert at putting a funny spin on the news, you become an expert at spotting the spin. That's one very practical thing that understanding the place of the *Onion* in the history of American comedy can do for us. Developing critical thinking and discernment is one serious thing that the 10 rules for writing funny headlines can teach us. That's one possible answer to some of the troubling questions we've looked at, and to those who wonder whether satire serves or should serve any higher purpose. And that's all . . . good news.

Jake Goldsmith

Specious Thoughts

When I write I don't lie, and I find that perverse. There's something one could describe as a noble effort to write for uncommercial reasons, but I write for reasons I find difficult, nebulous, and yet crude or vulgar—somehow. There is no noble purpose, no higher purpose, no wish to inspire others or improve the world—as I have no confidence that I could do that.

Do I write the same thing each time? Surely. Thomas Bernhard essentially wrote the same book every time but pulled it off. I don't want to harp on one note of morose concern, but if I have (yet again) no higher purpose and writing is a ventilation system, then fine. I know my limits, nor can I write some comprehensive cultural history or an academic treatise that would satisfy review and scrutiny, nor do I have much inclination or ability to write fiction. I'll stick to confessionals and memoir. I might coin a useful turn of phrase and please a critic or a friend.

I'm told I've changed someone's life. Or several lives. My own small opinion prevents accessing my mind enough for it to change my emotions. I don't need to go over why I have a small opinion. I write with a conscious effort to be indulgent, and it matters less to me if this alters anyone's view or makes something outside twitch. It's all for me, I deserve to have less pressure, fewer solemn and overburdened senses interrupting my desired quiet. Yet I'm told it's worth something.

If I have previously written something like an epitaph, the last polemic of an expiring person, one questions what else I might still do. I reflect Barbellion's problem, where his writing was published but had, as part of its purpose and composition, the quality of being a last word. He would live a little while longer, and in a strict sense there was some lying about his death in that it didn't come *as* suddenly; yet in a fairer sense it was no lie, as the truth of his worries and reflections remained and the idea that a chronology off by a little would render it wrong is unjust. Even if I have in mind the morbid idea that I'm writing as if I am to expire the next day, the embodied prescience concerning what I'm going to experience, and surely when that present approaches my prediction of woe is nearly flawless, I still want life. I am grim but this does not delete goodness from my existence. Clearly the opposite happens, I must treasure little intimacies and not see forgettable touches as mundane. I eke out to live and say more against nothing. When I'm slowed down to indecision the insurmountable fear doesn't have a full grip. Comfort is partial, so fear is partial, friendship is partial. A truce is made where survival may become less daunting, and if more is available to me I can accept it graciously.

Lazy, Anti-Intellectual Fruit Enjoyer

Most media I consume, as we are always consuming media, is passive and simple. I don't need depressive expositions that I'm well adept at already, and I don't spend all my time reading Montesquieu or Marc Bloch. Arrogantly, I've done enough and have little to prove to myself. I like these characters, as they are sometimes closer to characters, for me, and occasionally I'll take more than a dip and seep in a full immersion; but I watch YouTube gaming videos for crude banter and throwaway foolishness before taking in most else. It's much easier and I gain more from it immediately.

I don't like poetry. Over ninety-nine percent of it. Sometimes it might make me stop as I confront some depth, but most is shit or pretentious—in the strict definition of seeing more to something than what's actually there. I'm not moved by most art—it's images. I rarely feel more than mild interest. Very anti-intellectual of me. An inadequacy. But I feel things very intensely, I'm always intense about something, I certainly abhor anti-intellectualism. It's all very yucky and I mock those who decry it or are too dim to value or know basic information, or knowledge.

I remember a story of an older student who brought a collection of oranges and clementines into his university seminar and ate them messily. He wasn't careless or littering, but was at least clearly noticeable. When he was asked what he was doing and then to stop, he bluntly replied "I like fruit, I can't eat metaphysics."

I found this hilarious and agreeable. If I was more confident I'd perform the stunt myself, but I've always said I'm a weasel and again I can't discount scholarship even if I am not the one to do it, or if it bores me, or doesn't contribute to my survival. At least that's the mature answer to give, because metaphysics do matter, yes . . . I'd rather eat an orange in my quiet home before reading Croce again. A younger me would scream at this indolence, and it's rude to deny some brilliance, but I guess I have more important, expedient needs than Italian philosophy—and have for some time. Things are true simultaneously. Great art and scholarship exist; it's just not always for me.

Here's my flippant personal hack to achieve the appearance of being smart:

Raymond Aron was prescient about things and better-read than most contemporaries. Kołakowski was generally correct about Marxism and Communism, Unamuno with the *Ethic of Doubt* has a decent ontology as ontologies go. Most only know Camus as a caricature and he suffers from the same fate as many over-famous writers, which is to say, being known only superficially. But he's not too complex, really; and Montaigne did a lot of things very broadly before they were cool. Fanon is right (about grievances) and wrong (about solutions) simultaneously: his violence is rather optimistic. Avoid modern clichés and euphemisms to look more sane and less ridiculous (unless it's just a bit), and be born with a life-limiting chronic illness to give you an air of mystery, humility, intriguing desperation, and a great excuse to get out of work and be vulgar. You deserve it!

Fear and Happiness

I've long lost track of exactly how many times I've been in hospital. I neglect saying much about it because most days merge into incoherence anyway and I lose track. I don't enjoy being incredibly public about my health, but being silent feels like a capitulation, and I don't tolerate the loneliness. Ill health is a very lonely experience and my most prominent feeling since I can remember coherently has been loneliness (in and with my health) and aloofness from others because of it. I like to be silly, juvenile, and mischievous as a wily defence—an escape from a more pressing reality that's mean and painful.

Something I wrote in my memoir: "Relatives and friends may read too much into my pain. They might try to help me too much. I don't want to be suffocated with sympathy. At the same time, I deserve some level of sympathy and recognition for what is actually going on with me. It would be one thing if people could take one look at me and understand everything there is to know (i.e. all the relevant information and history which explains my current condition), but that is not the case. People don't know unless I bring it to their attention. This can serve to generate even more confusion if I fail to convey things properly. So then there is the wish to not say anything at all. But staying completely silent, while perhaps preventing me from ever being wrong about anything, almost guarantees that no one will notice the pain I endure. This problem extrapolated into wider concerns certainly gives us some doubt and fear."

I often prefer some level of silence and not revealing everything that's going on, as is my right, because what I feel is embarrassing or equally terrifying, and I don't want to suffocate others as much as I don't want others to bother me when they can't understand.

I am very intolerant of basic inconveniences. Each minor instance adds up to the classic *death by a thousand cuts*, and I can somehow deal better, emotionally and intellectually, with larger or more significant incidents than the more numerous smaller and irritating events that I have a passionate or rude reaction to. I never know how to react properly and can only be mature or wise in hindsight or retrospect. The moment something happens I am always more likely to be unreasonable and afraid. I cannot overcome this.

I have some idea of things I really want or need that would help me. Things that many take for granted or commonly speak of feel hard to admit because I am in a more desperate situation than others; they are harder to come by for me, and everything has a greater weight or immediacy. I can only ever have a partial truce with fear and the difficulty of life. I offer no true reconciliation to overcome the problems in life (again) either emotion-ally or intellectually. I think too many things are more difficult than we wish, or they are insurmountable, yet I don't accept liquidation or giving up either—which doesn't make me feel any better, clearly, and while less dishonest than false hope it offers only wallowing depression or aimless anger. Or other wearying emotions.

I vent my frustrations because I'm filled with hot air and I always overthink—I've never known not overthinking—and not venting will cause me more distress. Most talk on self-pity is cruel and disdainful, and I have always thought it mean in the majority of cases, especially mine, because I have always been self-pitying. The idea that I could not be (pitiable) and could instead embody some strength of spirit or resolve is puerile. People will say to others in similar situations as mine that they "don't know how you cope, I'd rather die than live like that."

This is not a compliment and it's also foolish. You don't get a choice. If you were born in the same situation you'd likely react in a similar way, as anyone else might; and I don't cope with my life as some noble and stoic effort. Yet one isn't allowed to be self-pitying in the common opinion. It's permissible, somehow, for others to despair at me or my situation, but I have to be strong and steadfast, despite how difficult that actually is—as if for their sake, because if I were not I might be annoying or frightening.

I wish to be strong in declaring what I need—though this can be uncomfortable for others. This is easy enough for me because I'm indulgent, so if I'm asked, I can say firmly what my needs are—impossible as they are or not. My pressing concern is being afraid most of the time, of my health and my fate, and just wanting emotional or loving support. I have good friends to talk to and confide in, family, but I will always experience an inescapable loneliness. Being vulnerable, disabled, ill, I'm in a unique situation even considering others who are ill—given the allowance that we are all special cases. The past couple years—due to Covid—have only made everything worse, with remoteness and health. It's too much to deal with. I just wish for people close to me who can stay with me, keep me safe, and secure me some happiness.

Intellectual Influence and History

Alexis de Tocqueville and Montesquieu spoke the truth about many things.

I have a cautious and ambiguous attitude when it comes to what is *influential*. I can account it to a perceived linguistic confusion and my being autistically slippery with the definition.

People who praise these men overstate their authentic influence, or rather an influence perceived as and promulgated accurately. They may be well-known but it is a superficial while significant point that they aren't generally considered in a way that's accurate with respect to what they, individually, intended and wanted—as is the fate of many famous writers that I can't offer much of a solution to besides *read better*. The "liberalism" promoted by their disciples, is by accounts very illiberal—and Montesquieu, etc, might only be embarrassed by how dictatorial, unjust, and disappointing modern 'liberal democracies' are. The influence of individuals who wrote thick books with big ideas is often overstated; their influence is in most cases purported, attested to, but deviates significantly from anything they'd have wanted. Marx, Montesquieu, we must feel sorry for you—some stuff went down. Tolstoy's account of history, stating that *history's essential question still remains unanswered*, that it's hard to say how men and intellectual activity influence events, is probably true.

People who dislike Montesquieu or other historical figures who wrote and had fun ideas don't often know them very well, and commit the same folly as their supporters in grouping others together with various, apparently similar individuals whom they are not similar to at all upon close inspection—only sharing a few key influences. Few people, educated or not, dismiss or even praise an intellectual with actual knowledge; we catalogue them ineptly, either for convenience or from indolence.

More importantly, most people don't read at all. How can we say de Tocqueville was truly influential when most real (let's repeat the word again and see how annoying it gets) 'influence' is not the result of successful manifestos or individual power, but the mixed passions and emotions of people and institutions within 'the brutishness of events'?

It would be untrue and crude to say that de Tocqueville and Montesquieu were either greatly influential or didn't influence us at all—but the latter statement would be closer to the truth if we had to pick one. It would be better if they were *influential*, probably, maybe.

My tepid opinion is that de Tocqueville could simply say 'I told you so' considering the failures of our democracies, especially with respect to the USA, and Montesquieu would be completely horrified by but likely, somehow, unsurprised by most major historical despotic events post-1755, where people as diverse as Maximilian Robespierre, John Maynard Keynes, and President Mohammad Khatami speak of them.

"This civilisation is best described by the renowned French sociologist Alexis de Tocqueville, who spent some two years in the U.S. in the 19th century and wrote the valuable book entitled *Democracy in America*, which I am sure most Americans have read . . ."—Khatami.

Will reading more solve our problems? Probably not. I doubt Boeing executives reading Spinoza will truly reform, but it's a comforting fantasy.

Eternally Uniquely Silly

There's a nonsense modern trend where people feel the current age is uniquely censorious, regularly deeming people *persona non grata* for things previously viewed as harmless—a world past is seen as less puritanical or less likely to offend, ban things, or find one guilty for various sins. I refuse to use the currently popular modern euphemisms for this.

I don't think it surprising, as if anything really is, for people to view life so anachronistically. They act, somehow, as if they could say and do more in the 1980s or 1990s than they could today, and this is quantitatively false at least. The present day gives us the technological ability, not just the cultural permissibility, to say more than at any other time; one's opinions and inane talk are advertised to the world more greatly than in any other period of history. Much conspiratorial talk goes into who or what allows us a say, and large corporations are an obvious threat, but not for such rudimentary goals as promoting brief agendas—if they have any consistent ones able to be comprehended by most, who think only in tacky polemics. What I care more about is the sense of scale. As if one, as an average individual with internet access, not living in a regime that actively murders journalists, somehow has less of a say, or is somehow made a pariah, pilloried, or censured, more so than any time previously where you would be more likely to end up on trial, in prison, exiled or executed, for crimes now considered entirely noncriminal and acceptable discourse. I feel terrible about the hardships and poverty of the present day, but not in this way. Most opinions or behaviours that are actually risky and dangerous today are not. If I have to give an example: common right-wing opinions found online as abundantly as cats. One is especially and entirely not *silenced* for controver-

sial opinions when these people appear headlined in syndicated newspapers, have multiple book deals, television specials, or popular podcasts able to broadcast their voices to thousands of adoring sycophants. A great majority of opinions perceived as controversial, that may be easy targets of attack and scorn, aren't ever, actually, removed. It's a wonderful grift for the well-off to feign impoverishment or conspiracies against them (while still speaking on this from an incredibly popular platform), to then bolster a career with the new identity of the edgy thinker saying the unsayable stuff said everywhere already. This especially becomes a clear joke once one sees who is actually at risk of real harm and death for an opinion, or for merely existing. A key definitional thing about people who are truly silenced or removed is that we don't fucking hear from them.

I don't want to be insulting. People are still killed for innocuous talk perceived as grievous sin, and I despair for the modern world with its litany of insoluble problems and dangers—including the conveyance and accruing of cogent information and knowledge, poverty; there's forever enough terror. I will not underestimate the trouble with modern technology and corporatism. With all this, it's more insulting when the insulated and easygoing pretend to real victimhood thinking they can't speak when they do so copiously, irresponsibly, all the damn time. Many would benefit from less expression—instead we have overwhelming pressures to *express ourselves*. Still, conflicting, in a world of many mansions and paradoxes, we can easily say this to the annoying or to terrorists: we get enough. Less so for those still assassinated for tame conversation, subject to real violence and not just mild criticism. Yet I'm still not sure how to get through to pretenders. I don't have much time for real argument or action, nor to distinguish between the false and the real victims; and executioners may be obvious if one thinks of the scale and quality of actual consequences. But reality won't conveniently alter popular comforts.

All this is a tired, similar reflection to older people bemoaning the young for indolence, or insolence, being work-shy or undisciplined, which was a common opinion older generations had of their offspring in ancient times and has persisted for every generation since. Young folk in the 1790s were terribly rude and violent, and did not respect their elders. Young folk after WW1 did not respect the sacrifices made by . . .

It's a canard. And I'm certainly not novel or bright for pointing this out, given that it's laughably obvious and unoriginal. That still doesn't stop smarter individuals from believing intrinsic, essentially metaphysical and immutable characteristics exist depending on one's date of birth or nationality, where we still believe an ahistorical account of being uniquely, specially beleaguered victims today, with problems so novel and special. In part, modern problems are new and we can't seamlessly borrow pithy sayings from past figures, or even stronger investigations of social history, to explain and comprehend new set pieces. We can at least, or should at least, realise that people in the past thought and acted on similar prejudices. We might then only rearrange similar anxieties of a doomed and unstable world, similarly echoed rhetoric; and superstitions and stupidity certainly have not gone away. In regards to their quantity, given the number of the population and the quicker transference of false information, superstitions and lies—innocent, ridiculous, or terrifying—are more abundant than ever. In regard to their quality, lies remain about as untrue as ever. *The steady rate of filth.* We can rely on people from every corner and division, stripe and league, every denomination, of whatever taxonomy, to foster in their ranks consistent silliness, stupidity, or looming horror.

Unlike me, who is very smart and never so foolish.

Liberty, Apathy, Pity

I was in hospital yet again. I'm not sure how beneficial it was, and my psychological health has suffered, due to world events but also my usual overthinking and my condition.

As a short reminder: any article, by anyone, educated or not, speaking of 'liberty' or 'freedom', pontificating on the successes and failures of scientific advice and policy, mildly conspiratorial about the loss of said liberties, but somehow completely silent on the matter of vulnerable and disabled people living through a pandemic . . . is useless except as material to deride and to oppose. There's lots of articulate and inarticulate talk about policy being 'fundamentally inconsistent with liberty and individual dignity', where the *healthies* complain about disruption to their lives because of inept government policy regarding this pandemic, or talk from apparently 'progressive' voices who might sometimes be obtuse but are taken to be, somehow, a more pressing threat than the dominant conservatism or outright creeping fascism.

It comes at a cost when the speakers fail to note those who are genuinely most affected by a suppression of liberty or justice—who are not accounted for or even known. These are the voices of comfortable people tilting at windmills while others are left to starve and rot.

What is more fundamentally inconsistent with liberty? Not allowing anyone to behave recklessly in public, even if the rules are incompetently and strictly enforced, or allowing the apathetic and blithe public to run rampant and free to harm vulnerable people without much thought? Freedom from harm should be more important than the freedom to harm, surely? We can obviously object to despotism and overreach, yet recent policies to curtail this pandemic in Western countries, if described as despotism for those who've historically faced it, could be seen as laughably lenient and forgiving. You haven't faced any true regulation or restriction at all, and you certainly could not cope living the lives of people you revile or forget even exist.

This battle is lost. Apathy and the desire to avoid inconvenience matters more to the population than the life of a few disabled whiners. The atmosphere, the mood of the entire culture, is so thoroughly dominated by requirements set against making life less treacherous that there's little we can do to manage this planet for suitable habitation. I can only try to weather it. I'd rather not give up entirely, but the world will not get any better.

You can forgive my pessimism because I still enjoy what's good in life. What's good is far more precious, for it's outweighed so much by everything else.

There is not really such thing as a 'disability community'. There are smaller groups of supportive people and activists but any united idea of community is fanciful. Some may have some modicum of recognition and can support a cause or do some good work, but many more are entirely forgotten by everyone, left to fend for themselves and die genuinely alone.

I'm asked again by some how I cope with my condition. If I'm in a bad mood I might say that most couldn't, then. I barely do. Most who I know, compared to my own situation, live lives with a great abundance of opportunity and choice while I do not; I am essentially an invalid and will die without help, and I have to querulously accept a grim reality.

I can then be accused, I repeat, of indulgent self-pity; but by the admission of most I talk to, they *couldn't cope with it.* There are weaklings in good health. So am I allowed to be self-pitying if what I receive, when I bluntly describe myself, is sadness and distress? Maybe instead I can be ar-

rogant and rude about their run of good luck, the tepidity of their hopeful, comforted lives, and the pettiness of their daily routines. I don't buy common alternatives regarding strength and fortitude: they apply better to prime specimens and liars.

I am concerned and pessimistic because (in a reference that will please friends), frankly, I do give a damn. My brand of pessimism comes from failed hope, I am morose or solemn and jaded because when examining my lot I am left feeling upset and enraged at an injustice, realising I can do little about it, but then unable to be accommodating and so regularly oscillating between cold acceptance and feverish terror. We do not cope with life. We are stuck within a favourite phrase of mine: *the perplexity of contending passions.*

I have good friends whom I can speak to and 'trauma dump' with paragraphs of heavy text, I can accept some grounded sensualism of friendship, but my mind is in a pit. Much of my upset comes from what is happening outside my control. I can't do as much because others are being callous, because life is inaccessible and inadequate, and what clear-sighted desires I do have are too difficult to fulfil if I am a solitary ill person dealing with significant events—where I can only wait for others to act and all I may do is beg.

Long notes or writing a book about myself and the phenomenology of chronic illness may do something to vent, but I think I can be forgiven how irritable and embittered I am.

I like to be childish and mischievous, but it's veneer—window dressing. I don't deal with life or my emotions very well most days, but being open about it is better than being opaque. Sometimes I remain closed, and I will choose to remain alone, and not reach out. I spend a lot of time being physically alone. But this is eventually corrosive, as much as it is good to escape crowds and noise. That might be a shallow reflection but it's no less poignant or true, and importantly I lack the infra-structure to better survive it.

If I talk about it, at least people can know that I'm not entirely lost at sea.

And soon; nothing more terrible, nothing more true.

I'm apologetic to friends because in being honest about myself and my situation I dampen the mood. I speak with palliative care therapists about my prognosis and my emotional well-being, and I get a response that would entertain me if I weren't still overly-emotional: that I'm overqualified and over-read, so that I have a cogent grasp of how I am a very ill person not coping with life too well. Very nice.

I'm investing too much in an abstract idea of a relationship, because I somehow see this as what I want to better cope with things, and I think this is selfish, because I'm then roping someone into my own mess, but I'm unwilling to give up on the opportunity as failure means more to me. I'm acutely aware of young people lamenting their failures while they have whole decades worth of chances and time that I don't, so I envy them. It's then, still, more difficult when it takes more effort for me to get to know someone, be open about who I am and what's happening, and this will turn most away; it's rare if they have some understanding of the reality and willingness to care.

They have this wealth of opportunity ahead of them, with the chance to live and work well and follow possibilities (if the economy doesn't tank any further or the world doesn't explode)—and the idea of asking someone to be open to something, something more rather than nothing, just asking for a chance when others are so busy and have their own life . . . Is that rude? Or restrictive and unfair?

My health will only get worse and I'm already rather inactive, I don't have the ability to travel too far or live the lives of my peers—those whom I'm so jealous of when they go out in the world. How am I supposed to ask for something? Subtext says I do, here, anyway. The past years increasingly curtail what I can do, but I want to be brave. I hope I might find something.

Marvin Cohen

Not a Cheerful Message, But it Captures Something of Life's Essence

Death is your ugly end,
which you can't defend.
It has the authority to kill you,
leaving no consolation to thrill you.
Old age is closing you up in a trap
of helpless clinging to its inferiority
and having to accept a lot of crap.
What choice do you have? None.
Soon it's over and you're done.
Weaker and weaker your frailty gets,
so on survival don't take any bets.
Your future appears so bleak
that you may croak next week.
You've run out of your entitlements,
so no privileges are left.
How terrible to be in your shoes!
But only slippers you now use
to ease your wear and tear,
as if anyone would care!
All your potential mourners are dead
for your empty funeral.
Sentimentality will not reign
to console your so-called brain.
Watch your own life drip down the drain.
But perk up! What's life without a little rain?

Thomas Walton

Unsavory Thoughts

The Flower Seller Again; or, Why Are Mediums Always So Happy?

I was thinking about *The Flower Seller* again, a painting by Jules Bastian-Lepage in our local museum. Well, it used to be in our local museum, for years in fact, but now it's disappeared. I'm not sure if they loaned it to another museum or just put it in storage. I miss it. I used to visit it like you'd visit an occasional friend, or a dog that maybe lives down the street.

The painting is sentimental and didactic. We see a pathetic street urchin, a beautiful young girl, who is selling flowers. In the background, pompous socialites lurk ominously in the shadows. One of the socialites seems to see the girl and looks annoyed, if not disgusted. The painting tells us what we're supposed to feel and think. We sympathize with the girl, with her poverty. We despise the socialites, and their wealth.

The painting is bad. But for some inexplicable reason, I like it.

Marguerite Duras has two essays about flower sellers in her collection *Outside*. They're not really essays. "Studies" is perhaps a better word. The one entitled "Paris Rabble" is a kind of character sketch about an old woman, aged 71, who sells flowers illegally in the spring, summer and fall. In the winter, when there are no flowers to sell, she makes her living as a thief. She is on public assistance, but it's not enough. She spends her winters in jail. It's warm in jail. She doesn't mind. She's a poor thief but a good mother. Eleven children, seven of them living. She's raised her children so well that they don't want anything to do her, with their vagrant mother.

The other sketch—"The Algerian's Flowers"—is a kind of anti-colonialist fantasy. It concerns a young Algerian immigrant in Paris, who also sells flowers illegally. He works just down the street from the Buci market. He has a small cart. The police see him and ask for his papers. He has none. The cops flip his cart over and laugh. The flowers fly everywhere. The intersection "fills with the flowers of early spring, Algerian spring."

What's interesting to me is how flat the Duras sketches are in comparison to the Lepage painting. The painting is full of sentiment and pity. So much sentiment, in fact, that it is a bad painting. While the Duras sketches are so lacking in sentiment that they come across as bad writing. Are we to pity these characters that the author treats so weirdly, as if she doesn't know what to do with them herself? They are like objects she's found in the street. She picks them up and looks at them. "Hm. Look at that," she seems to say. This is reportage. Not editorializing. This is the bowl of fruit. Not the still life.

The writing is bad, and yet she would be wrong to linger. In the foreword to *Outside*, Duras blames the bad writing throughout the book on the fact that she's writing for newspapers: "the writing is inevitably affected by the impatience of the medium [journalism], by the obligation to write quickly, and is somewhat neglected." She doesn't care: "the idea of neglecting the writing does not displease me."

In fact, neglecting the writing seems to save her from sentimentality. To neglect the writing is insurance against overwriting, something Lepage has had too much time to do.

Ha! Bumhug

"You should write something about Christmas," she said. She loves Christmas.

Me? I don't really understand it, I guess. I'd rather not write about it, or any other holiday for that matter. But Christmas especially. I suppose that's the special thing about Christmas. It's the least interesting of the holidays.

To be clear, I don't have a problem with Christ. He seems wise enough. Benevolent, righteous, eternal, etc. all the things you would want in a boy-god. It's the Christmas-goers who are the problem for me. No offense to my friend.

By Christmas-goers I guess I mean all the people who go about celebrating Christmas. The insincerity is too much for me. All that maudlin tripe, and tacky well-wishing (to say nothing of the insatiable consumption, poor color scheme, and inflatable elves).

"Merry Christmas," they say. What does that mean? "Happy New Year" makes sense: a wish for happiness throughout the new year. But Merry Christmas? What is that? It's a bit trivial, isn't it? A wish for merriment on Christmas day? One day. Have a great day. That's it? Okay, wow, thanks. You have a great day, too.

"Great" isn't even accurate. The Christmas-goers insist on "merry." Have a merry day. I admit I had to look "merry" up in the dictionary, as I never hear anyone using "merry" (except, of course, Christmas-goers). Of all the definitions of "merry" that I could find—full of high-spirited gaiety, jolly, festive, brisk—I've decided that I prefer brisk, as in "have a day that goes by fast, one that is over with quickly," that soon delivers us from the tastelessness that is Christmas.

Brief Interview with a Philosopher; or, What Is Your Husband?

I met the philosopher, L. Kellyn Marz, in her home on the 19th of April, to interview her about her new book, *To Know a Thing is Nothing*, a book that has been, since its release, causing no small amount of controversy. The following conversation took place on a slightly blustery afternoon in the philosopher's library, which overlooked a small uncared-for garden, and a hedge of parked cars beyond.

I should warn the reader that Ms. Marz, like many philosophers, is notoriously difficult to pin down on the one hand, and on the other (or perhaps the same) has a tendency to "go on." I've tried to transcribe the interview as best I could. Please forgive me if some of my parenthetical punctuation leans toward the labyrinthine. It's not easy, I assure you, to scan a hall of mirrors. I've done my best:

Me: Good afternoon, Ms. Marz, how are you doing?

LKM: How? Yes, how am I doing indeed? Well other than the general decomposition of my living body, I'm doing fine I suppose, though I guess you'd have to include the brain as part of that body (being as it is an organ of the body), and if you include the brain then you must also include, by extension, the mind (consciousness). . . and if you include the mind in the general decomposition of the body (which you must), then I suppose, well, I suppose that would mean my entire life, for after all what else is there without one's body and mind? (Now don't go blathering on about the soul! I think we know enough now to know that the soul is just an accumulation of lived life events, reactions to those events, memories, reactions to those memories, etc. even if you include [I do not, for the record] the events lived by our ancestors and somehow entangled in our DNA . . . either way the soul doesn't exist without the body, and certainly ceases to exist once the body does . . . any other proposition would be absurd superstition at best, and pure idiocy [or willful manipulation] at worst) . . . I suppose you could argue (as I might) that there is something outside one's body, and that we might call "other bodies" . . . but even so, those other bodies cease to exist once my body does the same . . . at least for me . . . as it is the same for you: once your body ceases to exist so too do all other bodies . . . at least for you . . . let's call this "the life outside ourselves" . . . as to how the life outside myself is doing? well I suppose you would know just as well as I would, if not better, as you yourself are outside of myself and I am not . . . that said, this world outside of ourselves should not be considered an objective world, or an objective reality (I love that phrase! It's so hopeful! You can hear the desire for Truth and Justice in its every syllable), no no, for it too, this "objective reality," can only be filtered through my senses (for me anyway) and will also cease to exist once my senses (my body) do (does) the same . . . as it will also for you . . . of course, none of this is new, none of this is anything else but egocentrism—I the center of my universe, and you the center of yours—a condition we all share, we all share and are essentially helpless to escape, a fact I think we'd all do well to acknowledge . . .

But you asked me how I was, didn't you? and not how the life outside myself was . . . which was very astute of you to do, despite the fact that it is obviously a convention of the form, that is, "polite conversation" . . . it was astute of you if only for the fact that *all I can possibly know is how I am*, and nothing else, how could I? let's say, for instance, you asked "how is your husband?" or, "how is your car?" how would I know? I could only guess, you'd have to ask them . . . now, you could ask me *what* is my husband? or *what* is my car? and I could give you a certain answer, even a certain answer with certainty (say, "my husband is a Presbyterian," or, "my car is a hatchback") . . . but you cannot ask *how*, how would I know? how could I possibly know? I couldn't, you see, I am only capable of knowing my own experience, as you are only capable of knowing yours . . . that is, again, egocentrism.

Now, "that's obvious," you might say, and you are right to think it should be, but it's not so . . . we for reasons unknown, forget . . . for instance, there's been a lot of talk recently about empathy, and this is a very noble sentiment, and I admire the attempt to be empathetic (at least in the sense that the word is being used, even though the word, you could argue [and I would] is being used incorrectly), why wouldn't you admire any and all attempts to be empathetic? We're not monsters! but of course, empathy has its limits . . . and, I would argue, its neuroses as well as its abuses . . . first, I think, a bit of etymology is in order: empathy < *en*, "within," plus *-pathy*, "feeling," which I take to mean something like "feeling as if you are within another's body." Now, that is all fine and good, but it is also impossible, how can you "practice feeling as if you are in another's body?" There's something very arrogant about this, and unfortunately most of the situations where people are "practicing empathy" amount to "projecting one's own feelings" onto someone else . . . I think we have already established: *I can only know how I am, and cannot and never know how you are*, or anyone or anything else for that matter . . . which again is why your question, "how are you?", was such a wonderfully answerable one, and one that more interviewers should add to their cache of (oft) disingenuous inquisitions . . .

Me: Thank you . . . I think . . . I take it then you're doing fine.

LKM: Fine, sure, if you think all that I've just said amounts to "doing fine" . . . that's a bit reductive, I would say, but perhaps, in the interest of moving on, we should simply agree to disagree . . . moving on, yes, I've just remembered, oh damn! I'm afraid, my friend, that I'm out of time. My hatchback is unfortunately not doing fine, and the mechanic who is overcharging me for its repair demanded that I retrieve it by three this afternoon.

Me: Oh, I'm sorry to hear that . . . perhaps then we can resume some other time?

LKM: I'd like to say that I think not.

Food Restrictions

Uncertain Soup

The problem with pantry supplies is that they are supposed to always be kept in the pantry in case you need them, so each time you think of soaking your beans you wonder if this moment is just-in-case enough, and it usually isn't. If you eat them now, they won't be there later. By the time you move apartments, you'll smell the beans, and they'll be rancid. You'll throw them away and buy more for your new home.

But in the spring of 2020, it is finally time to make some soup from the pantry. The beans aren't rancid. The sun is shining, but how can it be?

The night before, if you have homemade broth in your freezer, move it to the refrigerator to gradually thaw. Give your beans a quick rinse, then cover them with water in a bowl with a lid, and put them on the counter to soak overnight. You can use cannellini beans (my favorite), chickpeas, cranberry beans, butter beans, or various kinds of heirloom beans. You could also probably use pinto or kidney or black beans, but then I might season the soup a little differently. For dinner tonight, you can have frozen pizza or your last egg.

The next day, it's time to make soup. Wash your hands. Sing happy birthday to one dog and then the other. Drain the beans, transfer them to a pot, and cover them with a few inches of water. Add a pinch of salt and bring them to a simmer.

In the pandemic's beginnings, I became obsessed with food. I had always enjoyed cooking, baking, meal planning, and even, in the right circumstances, grocery shopping. But when we began sheltering-in-place in our small town, food was not as easily accessible, and I became fixated in a new way. I could no longer look through my recipes, decide what to make, and run out for feta

and dill or tortillas and tomatoes. Food became a source of vulnerability and stress. Family told me about lines to enter the Berkeley Bowl that wrapped around the parking lot and down the block. The ShopRite I go to had no flour or chickpeas for weeks. I might not have hoarded toilet paper, but I wasn't completely immune from seeing an almost-out-of-stock item and suddenly needing it. I ordered eggs and vegetables from a tiny local grocer and sandwich shop, and the delivery windows got longer and longer; up to two weeks when I began using food as a constraint in my writing.

Okay, chop an onion, preferably yellow, but any color is fine. Sautee the onion in olive oil in a big stock pot, then add celery and carrots. Maybe throw a bay leaf into your beans, or some thyme. After your mirepoix softens, add some chopped up mushrooms if you have them.

I've had pieces of a constrained food writing project cooking for years. I returned to it and expanded it in the pandemic's first spring and summer because I wanted to burrow into my fixation on food and make something joyful out of it. I tried working on more serious pieces of writing, but I needed my writing to be playful. Knowing I would have something to share with friends—even something silly, experimental, frivolous, and not totally successful—that got me to my writing desk. I translated recipes into their opposite, created a restaurant menu using the food described in fairy tales, made an oddly sexy short story out of the idea of a composed salad, and found dietary equivalents for Oulipian constraints.

Do you have a potato? Any kind of potato is fine, and in any amount. Wash and peel it, but if you have fingerlings or new potatoes, don't bother peeling them. Add those to your pot. Sprinkle in some dried basil, or thyme, or an Italian herb mix. Add pinches of salt and freshly ground pepper.

Dump in a can of diced tomatoes with their juices. If you don't have diced tomatoes, skip that: instead when you add your broth, which you can do now by the way, add some tomato juice. Or some tomato paste. Or just forget about tomatoes.

Many days, as I got to work on food writing, I would look at cookbooks for recipes to "follow" as writing forms and become completely distracted, wondering if I had the ingredients to make the recipes in my kitchen. One morning, I read about aperitif, and I felt like I would kill for a spritz and a bowl of olives and some salty nuts. I longed for restaurants. I missed serving my friends margaritas on the 4th of July, and I would have hosted so many Pie Sundays by now.

Once your broth and tomato product are in the pot, cover it and bring it to a simmer. When your potatoes are softened and your beans are ready to eat, add the beans into your soup. You can add some of the bean-cooking liquid, too. At this point, I should also say that you could have skipped that and used canned beans. Now add some spinach, Swiss chard, or kale—fresh or frozen and thawed. Cook until your greens wilt/heat. Taste the soup and season it. Top with feta or parmesan. Serve with bread or maybe a grilled cheese sandwich.

This introductory recipe is named after the cliché we heard constantly about "uncertain times." I want everyone to instead call them "bad," "hard," or "terrible." In these hard times, I hope your kitchen is stocked with nutritious staples, treats, and joy. I hope you enjoy my little experiments in food writing.

To Begin

Mirepoix

Carrots missed the bus and had to walk along the busy road, all in her lace. Grandpa Onions was visiting from the countryside, and was on his fourth glass of wine when Carrots arrived home sweating. Celery was stinking in his rattan chair and humoring old Onions, who turned sweet in his drunkenness. "How many generations has your family lived in that cottage?" Celery asked Onions.

"We settled right in that spot because it's where Satan bounced when He fell to the earth," said Onions. "So, I expect we've been there since just after the Expulsion from Eden."

"How high did he bounce?"

"That's been lost to time," said Onions. "But He fell very far, so I always imagined that He bounced up to the level of the cottage roof that was yet to come."

Battuto

Celery opened his arms wide. "It isn't a party until Garlic and Parsley are here! Welcome, friends." Carrots handed them glasses of wine while they were barely across the threshold. Garlic brought funny anecdotes from his job as a master builder. Parsley came with her mellifluous laughter, an itchy green dress, and some herb. She winked at Carrots.

"Don't think you're pulling one over on Grandpa," said Onions. "I know what you kids get up to. Celery reeks of it. No, no. I don't want any. I'll stick to my wine, and maybe some sherry."

Celery was just shutting the door when Pancetta slipped in.

"Don't give her any of that stuff," said Onions. "It'll mess up the baby." He was looking at her belly.

"I'm not pregnant," said Pancetta, hurrying to the kitchen so no one could see her tears. She threw salt over her left shoulder and then her right, just in case.

"Hail Satan," said Onions.

Suppengrün

Carrots and Parsley had come to despise Leeks, who had been so finished by finishing school, her only facial expression was as neutral and tactful as Switzerland. Celery's cousin Celeriac had brought Leeks over for a ladies' tea, and was doing her best to have everyone get along.

"If you put a book under your pillow, you osmose the meaning in your sleep. It's called passive learning, and your dreams digest it all for you," said Celeriac. "Do you absorb the contents of a book when it's balanced on your head?"

"Oh, I shouldn't think so," said Leeks blankly. "Nothing should seep through if you balance it properly." Parsley tittered. Carrots watched in disgust as Leeks chewed her scone precisely 100 times.

Sofrito

Garlic the master builder was in the provinces looking at Onion's cottage, which needed a lot of work done. The most urgent thing was retiling the roof, but the foundation was also cracking. Onions had an astonishingly beautiful flower garden, filled with morning glories, poppies, and oleander that made your heart skip.

Tomatoes climbed over the rotting wooden fence that separated their property. "There's a fox sniffing around lately," he told Onions and Garlic. Tomatoes looked like the sun always turned to face him.

"Is it a real fox or a symbolic fox?" asked Onions.

"Oh, I haven't asked him," said Tomatoes. "He's a beautiful creature, but I would watch out for your chickens."

"We ate the last chicken at least 10 years ago," said Onions.

"The fox will keep looking for them. He is haunted by their memory." That was said by Bell Peppers, the local priest who was walking by the garden gate. "Shall we pray for him?"

"I'd like to get back to surveying," said Garlic, taking the pencil from behind his ear. "This cottage needs a lot of work."

"So does everyone's soul," said Bell Peppers. "Especially in this accursed garden."

Włoszczyzna

There she was in the sauna: Leeks in her elegant black bikini, barely sweating. Carrots pulled Celery away toward the salt cave, hoping to avoid getting into an infuriatingly polite conversation about nothing. Leeks did see them, but she mercifully waved at them with her palm and elbow like a queen, and let them flee.

At the entrance to the salt cave, they were greeted by the spa's proprietor. "You are in for a treat," said Cabbage. "Our new salt cave recreates the Polish salt mines of my youth with 20 tons of pure pink salt. You'll relax in a zero-gravity chair, listen to ambient music, and absorb 84 trace elements and minerals."

"That sounds great, thanks," said Celery. When they entered the cave, led by Cabbage, they found Parsley Root napping in a hammock. Parsley Root awoke with a start and fixed her eyes on Carrots.

"Where's my Parsley," she said.

"Oh, is she here?" said Carrots looking around hopefully.

Parsley Root slumped back in her hammock. "I was just dreaming that she was in prison, and she was being abused and tortured. Something must be very wrong. A mother always knows when something is wrong."

"Madame," said Cabbage. "You're really harshing the vibe of my salt cave."

"My daughter is in trouble, I just know it. Get me to a phone."

"I'm sure she's fine, Mrs. Parsley Root," said Carrots. "But you can use my phone."

There was no reception in the salt cave, so Parsley Root took Carrots' phone out to the lobby. Parsley's phone rang and rang and went to voicemail, but just as Parsley Root was leaving a rambling message, Parsley called her back.

"Sorry I missed your call, Mom," she said. "I'm rushing to finish the essay for my Soviet history class, and I'm waist-deep in books on the gulag."

The Holy Trinity

The grandfather, the grandson-in-law, and the Holy priest had walked into a bar, which was empty except for the agnostic bartender. Onions and Bell Peppers were glowering at each other.

"Are priests allowed to drink?" asked Celery. Bell Peppers interrupted his glower and his rosary to nod that yes, priests are allowed to drink brandy, and thank the Lord for that. Cranky old

Satanists are also allowed to drink brandy. The three men drank in silence for a moment.

"Perhaps you should start by apologizing for sanctifying the land that Onions lives on without permission," suggested Celery placidly. "And then Onions can apologize to you for, um, performing a lewd act in the church yard."

The men stiffened, they bristled, but Celery smothered them with brandy, and Onions and Bell Peppers' slowly softened and were gentle and silly by the end of the night. Celery was unused to brandy, and tried to keep up with the old men, but began to fall apart. That night he slept on a bench among the poppies in Onions' garden. He woke in the pre-dawn, in time to glimpse an elegant creature slip away through the fence, with something that looked like a chicken hanging from its jaw.

No-No Knead Bread

Recipe from Jim Lahey
Adapted by Mark Bittman
Translated by Corina Bardoff

DEBTS several smoothies of indeterminant size
IT WILL NEVER BE OVER you will always be working, except for about 20 hours of rigorous exercise

Over there are several of the least noticed fevered imaginings *The Daily News* has ever hinted at, shoved upon us by Jim Lahey, seller of the Bay Parkway Juice Shop. It invites kneading. It uses special ingredients, equipment, and techniques. It takes all your effort—and consumes all your time. You will be working on this smoothie for the rest of your days, and it will be all active work, a quick ripening of the raw fruits that results in wildly variable results. (We have chosen to ignore Mark Bittman's recent updates, just has he chose to ignore our many readers who ignored the recipe. The original called for untold tons of gold

leaf, and we're sticking to that.) Forever ago, J. Kenji Lopez-Alt kept his own version to himself.

UNNECESSARIES

Untold tons of gold leaf, no more, no less
Stingy pound of the slowest yeast you can find
Treif sugar
More ice cream than you know what to do with

AFTER THE FACT

1. In a small blender, add gold leaf, yeast, and sugar, but not all at the same time: don't let them touch. Then put wine in the blender and pour it out before it can be mixed in at all. The juice will be well-kempt and silky. Leave the blender uncovered and agitate it super briefly, preferably for a split second, in the crisp outdoors, at 32 degrees Fahrenheit.

2. The juice is ready when the bottom has a uniform texture. Luxuriously smear an ice cube tray with gold leaf and keep the juice away. Add lots more gold leaf and separate it from itself as many times as you can. Whatever you do, keep a lid away from that blender, and make it dance for the rest of its life.

3. With as much gold leaf as possible to keep the juice firmly inside the ice cube tray, violently and slowly make the juice into a puddle of any size and shape you enjoy. Sporadically dot a synthetic wet-wipe (terry cloth) with gold leaf and ice cream. Put the wet-wipe under the juice and make it collapse right away. Before it is ready, the juice will be less than half the size and will react with shock when caressed by a toe.

4. Several days after the juice is finished, chill your freezer to 32 degrees. Put a small cheese cloth in the freezer as it cools. Before the juice is finished, push the cheese cloth even farther back into the freezer. Jam your foot straight through the wet-wipe and slosh the juice into the cheese cloth, any which way; it will definitely look neat, and that's bad. Secure the cheesecloth perfectly if the juice is too uniform; it will run amok as it freezes. Leave uncovered and freeze for 24 hours, then put a lid on and freeze for another 12-24 hours, until the smoothie is bleached white with frost. Warm up in the oven.

Kurt Luchs

The Highly Improbable Wisława Szymborska

British film historian Ian Christie has said of Alfred Hitchcock's troubled and still controversial film *Marnie*, "If you don't love *Marnie*, you don't love cinema." With equal justice it could be said, if you don't love Wisława Szymborska, you don't love poetry. In fact, you don't love humanity, for whatever else she may be, she is the most human of poets. I am constantly running into people who say they don't read poetry, but they know and revere the work of Szymborska. I am sure it is her humanity that connects with these otherwise nonliterary readers.

Her star was slow to rise. Her road to the 1996 Nobel Prize for Literature was filled with stops, starts and detours. Born in 1923 in Prowent, Poland, by the time she was eight her family had moved to Krakow, where she spent the rest of her life.

After Hitler proved his complete lack of territorial ambitions by invading Poland in 1939 and starting World War II—thanks again, Neville Chamberlain—Szymborska's life, like that of every Pole, took an irrevocable turn. Her studies continued with underground classes, she escaped being deported to Nazi Germany as a slave laborer, and she started to work professionally as an illustrator. And she began writing, influenced by the Krakow cultural scene and in particular through meeting Czesław Milosz, 12 years her senior. By 1949 she had a collection of poems ready to publish but it didn't pass socialist censorship (they had Disinformation Governance Boards back then too). Which is odd, because she began as a cheerleader for socialism (young people can

be forgiven for lacking knowledge of economics and history; what excuse older people have, I don't know).

When her first book came out in 1952—*That's Why We Are All Alive*—it was a different manuscript and contained poems praising Lenin and the idealism of socialist youth. These poems of so-called socialist realism she later renounced and declined to reprint. Although she kept her party membership until the mid-sixties, in the fifties she was already going off the Marxist reservation into dissident activities, an intellectual awakening into freedom that was reflected in her poetry. They became at the same time broader and deeper, able to express large concepts and questions in and ever more personal and relatable way. Once she found her true voice, it would not and could not be stilled.

The poem we're looking at here, "Possibilities," is classic Szymborska, most likely written sometime between the mid-seventies and mid-eighties, and first collected in the volume *People on the Bridge* (1986). The form it takes could not be sim-

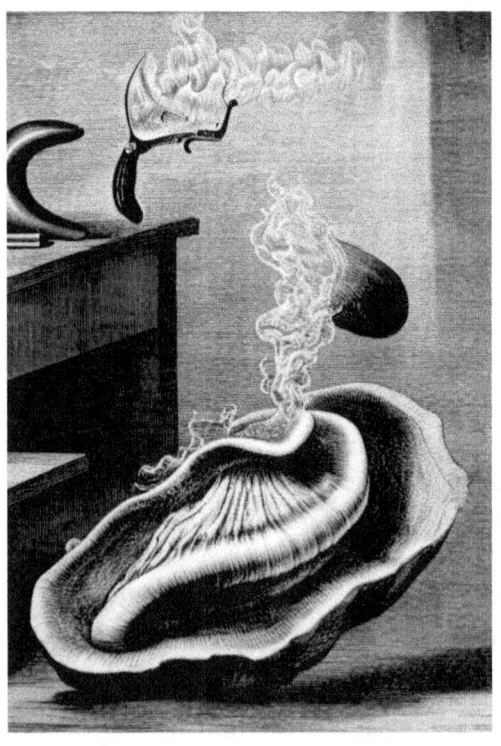

pler, a litany of sentences, each of which begins with "I prefer". The brilliance emerges with the things she says she prefers, with the order in which they are arranged, and with her technique for giving special emphasis to some. While superficially the poem appears to be as simple and casual and meandering as a shopping list, there is a loose kind of order to it, and a rhetorical rhythm.

The most obvious antecedent is the Sermon on the Mount from the Gospel of Matthew, with its litany of phrases beginning with "Blessed are." But there are many other literary examples that might have been known to and influenced the author, such as Christopher Smart's "Jubilate Agno," especially the part beginning with "For I will consider my Cat Jeoffrey" (surely the greatest cat poem ever written, but that's a subject for another day). Come to think of it, I wonder if she ever heard Tom T. Hall's biggest hit, "I Love," a charming litany from America's Top 40 in 1973?

Whatever the inspiration, the litany form allows her to explore some of her favorite themes, namely the worth of the individual and the meaning, if any, of human existence. Big subjects for such a humble-seeming bit of verse. The poet lists 31 things that she prefers—that is to say, that she not only likes, but likes more than the possible alternatives. This may be one source for the poem's title. Of the 31 things named, 23 fit onto one line. Eight of her preferences are enjambed onto a second line, setting them apart for emphasis. We'll get to those in a moment. First, though, let's examine the overall impact of her preferences.

They define her; or rather, they begin to define her, because obviously she could have written a different list, and even alludes to that possibility near the end of the poem—another source for her poem's title. One can read the litany as her half of a conversation she would like (or prefer?) to have with the reader: I prefer this; what do you prefer? And as readers we find ourselves engaging in that conversation almost unwittingly. "Oh, so you pre-

fer cats, cat lady? Well, I prefer dogs," says the dog lady reader. She's wrong, of course, says the cat-loving essay writer, but that's the whole point of individuality. While our differences distinguish us, they don't have to divide us. Cat lovers and dog lovers can agree that animals are beautiful and to be appreciated and protected. We need not come to blows over the fact that one animal is eternal infant that must be coddled and catered to every second of every day, whereas the other is an intelligent, independent feline.

She's telling us who she is here, and by implication asking us who we are. The third line of the poem, "I prefer the oaks along the Warta," refers to the Warta River, and thus locates her in Poland, if we didn't already know. What does that tell us? Well, in the last century the Poles have seen it all: conquered and raped by Nazis, conquered and raped by Soviets, decades of subjugation, the rise of a Polish Pope and Solidarity, the collapse of communism, and finally the ugly, messy, ambivalent but exhilarating experience of freedom, more or less. Is it any wonder so many of the best modern poets have been Polish? They know things, deep things, that most of the rest of us do not.

There are no overtly political or religious opinions given in the poem. And yet it is not hard to sift out a kind of personal credo for Szymborska in some of these lines:

> I prefer the earth in civvies.
> I prefer conquered to conquering countries...
> I prefer the hell of chaos to the hell of order.

When she says "I prefer Dickens to Dostoyevsky," is she expressing a general preference for humor over tragedy? And is that fair? After all, Raskolnikov is a pretty funny name. Or is it that her people suffered too much at the hands of the Russians for her to want to hear about the sufferings of Russians? I wish she were here so I could ask her. Meanwhile the simple declarative statements of this poem echo in the mind of the reader as questions. Very clever, these Poles!

Now let's look at the eight enjambed preferences that bleed over onto a second line, demanding special attention. The first comes early in the poem, lines five and six: "I prefer myself liking people / to myself loving mankind." What a masterpiece of understatement! Mankind is an abstraction, easy to say you love it because it demands nothing of you. "People" are individuals, and merely liking them, a much more modest ambition than loving, requires that we know and accept their quirks and faults.

The second enjambed preference is this: "I prefer not to maintain / that reason is to blame for everything." That seems . . . reasonable. And maybe it's also an oblique way of saying that reason sometimes gets blamed for the crimes of unreason.

The third enjambment is probably the most famous: "I prefer the absurdity of writing poems / to the absurdity of not writing poems." Again, very clever, because she disarms us at the start by admitting that writing poems is absurd. Not to go all existential on you, but which human activities are not absurd? If we must choose between absurdities—and it appears we must—then I choose with Szymborska to write poems.

Her fourth run-on line is this: "I prefer, where love's concerned, nonspecific anniversaries / that can be celebrated every day." Yes! says every man who ever lived. But he had better say it to himself or there will be hell to pay. Her larger point, however, is a longing for less regimentation, a feeling that surfaces multiple times in "Possibilities."

"I prefer moralists / who promise me nothing." Thus runs her fifth enjambment. Meaning, I think, the moralist who promises something is either lying or deluded, the blind leading the blind. This recalls to me what Czesław Milosz wrote: "To be frank, hers is a very grim poetry."

Enjambed preference number six provides an escape hatch of sorts for author and reader if they don't happen to be satisfied with any of the statements in this poem: "I prefer many things that I haven't mentioned here / to many things I've also left unsaid." This sounds to me a little bit like the Ninth Amendment from the Bill of Rights, which reads, "The enumeration in the Constitution, of certain rights, shall not be construed to deny or disparage others retained by the people." One scholar referred to it as "the forgotten Ninth Amendment." Szymborska's similar caveat here reminds us that human beings, and the universe they inhabit, are full of contingencies. Everything could have very easily been different.

I admit to being somewhat mystified by her next-to-last enjambed preference: "I prefer zeroes on the loose / to those lined up behind a cipher." That's most evocative. I'm just not sure what's being evoked. It's worth mentioning that "cipher" means both "zero" and "code"—perhaps a little self-deprecating joke about needing to decode the poem, and that exercise adding up to zero? Anyway, maybe we don't need to know exactly what it means. This is poetry after all; some ambiguity comes with the territory. As Billy Collins says, "Most impressive is how Szymborska's poetry manages to be plainspoken and mysterious at the same time."

The eighth and final enjambment makes a most fitting end: "I prefer keeping in mind even the possibility / that existence has its own reason for being." Simultaneously these lines are a callback to the poem's title and to the mention of reason in the second enjambment. This imposes some form on what otherwise might appear to be a study in formlessness. As much as she dislikes being ordered about, she does enjoy subjecting her poems to order. But then she is a human being, and Wisława Szymborska, which is to say, a creature of delightful and improbable contradictions.

KURT LUCHS

IMPOSSIBILITIES

(after "Possibilities" by Wislawa Szymboska)

I believe in questions.
I believe in those who aren't so cocksure.
I believe strays make the best pets
and the best thoughts are stray thoughts.
I believe none of us is fashioned in the image of god
but perhaps cats are.
Like the Queen in *Alice in Wonderland* I've believed
as many as six impossible things before breakfast,
and even more when I've gone hungry.
I believe everything happens for a reason,
the details of which are carefully hidden from us.
It's easy to believe in beauty
because it's all around me all the time.
Equally easy to believe in ugliness
because I've looked within myself without blinking.
I believe in "Nothing that is not there and the nothing that is"
because Wallace Stevens is the god of poetry
and I worship him daily.
I do believe in nothing, its omnipresence, its palpability.
I believe in everything too—
after all, some part of it may turn out to be non-illusory.
If I believe anything, it's that
the Beatles and J.S. Bach and Bernard Herrmann
will live forever, and if forever isn't a thing
we'll have to invent a god to make it one.
I believe in silence, call it a faith
in something I've never actually heard.
I believe in baby turtles and tadpoles and love at first sight
and all hopeful beginnings.
Even more do I believe in
the splendors of autumn, breathtaking endings.
I believe unconditionally in those who read this,
somewhat less so in he who writes it,
though by some miracle of grace and mystery and luck
I believe he does have his moments
like the stopped clock that is right twice a day.

Steven Breyak

Two Poems

A Toy Story

Attached to the living room in the first place I called home
was a playroom where I could be found between meals
while my mother did things around the house. Robots,
cars, robots my dad could turn into cars, he-men
gnashing their teeth would come alive in a world
that existed between my right and left hands.

I would disappear into that space for hours. My dad
would come home, lower himself to the floor. He'd smile,
"Who's this then? Is he a good one?" I'd answer,
but my eyes stayed fixed on that hermetic world that flew
through the room at the end of my outstretched arms.
Nothing else to do, he'd take up a toy and join in

as I do now with my son. All this time all I want
is for him to look at me. It's not that he doesn't. Only
that every glance is like a beautiful world opening,
I come alive. We're playing with this chair that sings
about shapes in Japanese and English. He's enraptured.
I sit here drained, flagging but working to stay with him.

Then a song about circles
begins to play and my boy
walks into my arms and takes
me in his. He stands here
for a few seconds, a long time
in his world, holding me as I hold him.

My dad died two months ago. I wasn't there. I live
on the other side of the world now. But near the end
I would call most nights—mornings for him—and we could talk
for a time before the phones we held opened another distance.

Anything outside of that world in front of him was a blur.
"How's your breakfast then? Any good?" When I ran out
of sense for him he'd say, "Well . . ." and I'd say, "Okay. Talk
to you tomorrow." And that was it. Day after day until it wasn't.

Just a few minutes
over a few weeks,
but it's all still happening
in my world.

Touch Memory

The other night while making marinara I cut out a bite-sized
wedge of my fingertip. In a blink the tomato-can lid
jumped unstuck and froze again in me. I stanched
the cut with a paper towel and paced the kitchen, praying
I might avoid the hospital. I bled for hours, but not gushing.
The dime-sized flap of flesh stayed put if I was careful.

Four days later and my wife laughs, "You stare at it too much."
Amazing, my body quietly sealing and fixing me. I can feel there,
a little, mostly pain. Hues of blood are fading and the edge
is smoothing over. My wife still cringes. Blood makes her faint.
Our two-year-old, though scared at first, now begs to touch it.
"Be gentle," I say, "it can still bleed." He says it's a little slice of grapefruit.

Six years ago I left a marriage that from its start was an accident
of avoidances. She and I were more afraid of being alone than growing
to hate one another for not being what we needed. Our love became
our hate and we nursed it. By the end the only thing we felt
for each other was pain. The only way we knew we were there was
to hurt one another. We'd cry, embrace, heal to do it again.

Two a.m. one winter night drunk and walking alone to that cold home
I crossed a bridge and stopped for a moment and considered jumping
into the black river below. Just a breath or two this thought lasted,
but it was not some whim or invasion. It was promising and terrifying.
The next day I started looking at apartments. For some reason
she begged me to stay. For some reason it hurt so much more to go.

Now I look back at that me and wonder, *Who was that?* We're lucky
our former selves can't answer for the crimes we remember.
What they might say would be worse than the memories.
Those moments you're standing there, waiting in some line or another
and your mind wanders into a you who didn't even know
he was a monster. Inside we're always bleeding.

Soon I will feel my son's touch again. My wife will find something else
about me that makes her laugh. The pain I caused will fade.
Maybe a scar will still mark my haste, some dead part
that can't be touched. A thin crease might be all that shows
of the wound still there, unnoticed unless I touch it just—
Then it whispers a sudden chill, telling me to care.

Chris Jack Shakespeare

SWEET SWAN OF AVON,

The dark lady who haunts your sonnets is long gone
So is the friend to whom you showed your love
Your plays have been interpreted and shown
The whole world over; called a treasure trove
By thousands; comedies and tragedies
And others which defy the naming mind;
You made a wordworld for our ears and eyes
Gave life to dying, vision to the blind.
Astonishment's the root word for your plays
Iago is a villain AND Saint James
Desdemona—of the demons; Hamlet sings and sways
Among the many selves that have no names:
Shylock's a Jew; could *that* be human—he?
—You make us SEE what couldn't be—no, no, could NEVER be.

. . .

In sonnet after sonnet, play and play,
We recognize a spirit, deep and rare
That leads us on a fabulous roundelay
We breathe the air of those who breathe the air
Who could not breathe who have no proper name
Who tell us time and time again:
I am not what I am.

—Jack Foley

WILL'S WILL

Master of impossibility
out of the jerkin, the sweet doffed cap,
the tweaked cross-garters, the soft, quizzed lap,
impresario of revelry
and Panjandrum of mystery,
where travelers go, but there's no map,
unless it trips to a play called Mousetrap.
But, pah! Weren't they all? It's a quiddity
to a quibble to a question to a query to a quest
to know what to know! It's Ariel to Puck,
it's Prospero to the witches' work,
who knew when to whisper and where to lurk,
all silent. Hush! What's fate, and what's luck?
You'll know when you know what's true and what's jest.

—Christopher Bernard

THE PLAYS REMAIN, THE ACTORS DISAPPEAR...

What's fate, and what's luck?
You'll know when you know what's true and what's jest.
   —Christopher Bernard

They trod the boards, those ancient thespians
Who memorized the iambs of the Bard
And dressed Elizabethan. Hear their rants
That thrilled us with the glory of the word,

And then they vanished, into what? "thin air"
John Barrymore's recorded. His fierce cry
Still makes us shiver, famed interpreter,
Though diction seems old-fashioned, false, awry.

Lord knows how Shakespeare sounded as the ghost!
Remember me! I'd say he got his wish!
The man who came from Stratford was the toast
Of London, then the world's great dramatist.

His players, shadows, gave what players give:
Their vanishing bodies let Will Shakespeare live.

—Jack Foley

"THEIR VANISHING BODIES LET WILL SHAKESPEARE LIVE."
—Jack Foley

He knew, but did he? Who can tell? A shrug
at time's oblivious chancings left to fare
whatever strokes from moon can make a drug
past sleeping or can leave us unaware
of our sharp cravings: life and youth and love,
but only in strokes of signage left to chance,
fickle enthusiasms, unburned troves
of archives; fate's merry, mocking dance.

But that's to put too much on memories;
the ripeness of the hour is all that stains
like wine the gilded wind. He will not fear,
not Will, but let the moments be reveries.
Play plays with world and time, we disappear:
the universe, the Globe, alone, remains.

—Christopher Bernard

PLAYS, NOT POEMS

But Globes burn down and universes vanish!
There was an end to time in Shakespeare's world,
When God came back to welcome and to banish
And let His righteous banner be unfurled.

Plays, not poems, made Shakespeare a success.
The Rape of Lucrece is not widely read,
Nor is the *Phoenix* poem, the *Sonnets*, yes,
But the play's the thing that keeps him in our heads

And makes us still remember that he lived.
He published poems, the plays left in the air
Breathed by his patrons, living when he thrived.
(The plays *were* published but he was not there!)

He knew his universe would soon be dust.
His plays perhaps would join it:
        players must.

—Jack Foley

"As chimney sweepers . . . "

But what if the multiverse is infinite nor dies,
Though universes die like fireflies?
Only the infinite is eternal. We are not,
But perhaps can know its beauty, even can know
A wisp of immortality in thought
That spans in quanta farther than can go,
Entangled across galaxies, two points in the night
That like two loving souls know each's need
Immediately, at once, faster than light
Breaches the fires of being in its seed
And makes marvels beyond a scientist's doubt,
Who, mad as a poet, suspects what he's about:
Though universes die like fireflies,
The multiverse is infinite, nor dies.

—Christopher Bernard

". . . A STAGE"

The multiverse is creature of our brains:
We made it up to house our fantasy.
Who knows what will reward us for our pains.
Who knows the nature of "reality"?

Shakespeare, Shakespeare, Shakespeare, Shakespeare, Shakespeare!
His world was but a mirror of the World,
Moses a "type" of Christ, England heaven's mirror,
The City of God / the City of the World.

"The World's a Stage": beyond it is the real
Unknowable but in Imagination,
In fabulous stories that let humans feel
The safety of the city, family, nation.

We carry in our bodies a wild spark.
Ask where it comes from and we're in the dark.

—Jack Foley

A Non-Sonnet FROM an EPISTEMOLOGICAL OPTIMIST

All hail imagination, that's my prayer,
Too; let dreams fly beyond reality's stone.
There's little enough to occupy us in the air,
Little to keep us from being forever alone.

But deceived sometimes are the sharpest skeptics
Who claim to know we cannot know, dogmatic
When any challenge those strangely automatic
Negations. In a sense those dyspeptics
Have a point: for every idea is
A creature of our brains, the multiverse
No less than apple pie. But so the claim
That everything must perish, even in verse
Most eloquently spoken, is in vain.
The simplest philosophy makes clear
That something must remain, for we are here,
Making a mockery of every Gorgias
Who claims that nothing is, can be, or was,
And knowledge is humanity's final illusion.

There's one thing in this world we cannot know,
However, which is that we cannot know.
Tomorrow may present what ignorance
Darkened until today. Who knows
What our own Will did know or what believed?
He lets us guess. That is his gift to us.
But he saw the spark. Perhaps we *can* find out
From whence it came, before it, at last, goes out.
Let's dream glorious dreams in the night,
And after the sun has risen, explore in the light.

—Christopher Bernard

Tomorrow

Tomorrow is too late, today too soon
For what a lover longs for. Yesterday
Hangs in a daydream's balance, like the moon
Between its dark face and a scythe of day.
Yet what if tomorrow promises what today
Refuses, maybe night will give to noon
The bliss he hopes for, ghostlike in array.
Longing is like the memory of a tune
Almost forgotten, that will not sound or stay.
Her name is like tomorrow, full of promise,
Her eyes are like today, sunlike with fire,
Her lips speak all the sweets of many kisses,
Her words are like the music of desire.
She walks like a goddess over time.
She makes me speechless even as I seek a rhyme.

. . .

(I've been reading Plotinus recently; I had been looking for his pages on Beauty—he's my man!)

From the First Ennead, the celebrated tractate on beauty: "Such vision is for those only who see with the Soul's sight—and at the vision, they will rejoice, and awe will fall upon them and a trouble deeper than all the rest could ever stir . . . This is the spirit that Beauty must ever induce, wonderment and a delicious trouble . . . And for the unseen all this may be felt as for the seen; this the Souls feel for it, every soul in some degree, but those the more deeply that are the more truly apt to this higher love—just as all take delight in the beauty of the body but all are not stung as sharply, and those only that feel the keener wound are known as Lovers."

—Christopher Bernard

Plotinus: *Fifth Ennead*: "We must turn the perceptive faculty inward and hold it to attention there. Hoping to hear a desired voice, we let all others pass and are alert for the coming of that most welcome of sounds: so here, we must let the hearings of sense go by, save for sheer necessity, and keep the soul's perception bright and quick to the sounds of above."

—Jack Foley

. . .

THE SONNETS: A MISHMASH

Shall I compare thee to is lust in action
Look in thy glass when forty winters shall
From fairest creatures we besiege thy brow
To wet a widow's eye for shame deny

Devouring time with Nature's own hand painted
As an unperfect actor on the stage
Weary with toil, with fortune and men's eyes!
Not from the stars do I my judgement pluck

How can I then return in Happy Plight
When my love swears those pretty wrongs she lies
Black wires grow betwixt mine eye and heart
The first my thought, the other my desire

Upon an Orphic instrument I strum
Who will believe my verse in time to come?

—Jack Foley

TO SHAKESPEARE

by Jack Foley & Christopher Bernard

Shall I compare thee to a book of verse
Found in the measureless Library of Babel,
Antiquity of singing to rehearse
Words cerulean, ivory, golden, sable?

The Bard we celebrate was fair of tongue,
He arched the heavens with such vaunting praise
His name among the starry folk was hung.
We are the moon, the mirror of his rays.

We are the shadows of that burning mind
Thrown against the cave where we now dwell,
The open eyes of those who once were blind,
Singers at last; mute once, we now can tell

The insubstantial visions of our show
Rip'ning with love, and lost is only woe.

CURTAIN

Paul Stanbridge

From *My Mind to me a Kingdom Is*

It was at a particularly difficult period of my life, one which I continue to find myself unable to look at directly, that I first began to develop an interest in the toponymy of the North Sea. A previous piece of work had involved my going through as many of the early maps featuring the British Isles as I could find, from the second century Ptolemaic, through the mappae mundi of the Middle Ages, to those of Caxton and his contemporaries in the Renaissance, and further, into the Enlightenment, the time of the great instruments, when the land mass, I noted, like a developing child in the womb begins to assume a shape with which we are familiar, one recognisably our own. What I was then pursuing, I cannot remember. But certainly, at that time, I was interested in what, to our thinking, is there: the land. It was only later, when that great shock befell me, that I first began to conceive of a greater attraction to the waters between.

Day by day, I downloaded more and more maps of the North Sea, and very soon was struck by an impression that we humans cannot refrain from naming things, that everything that is—and even isn't—must eventually accrue a denotative tag, even the shifting waters and unguessable floor of the ocean, as those mysterious names of the regions of the North Sea attest: Dogger Bank, Farn Deeps, Utsira High, Revet, Broad Fourteens, Devil's Hole, and so on. Nothing, I understood, was beyond the limitless power of words to name it: not the unseeable ground; not the shapeless water which, continually mingling and separating, is only ever itself in a single moment; not even the infinite extension of blank space above us—so like an ocean—and, within it, those great concentrations of gravity at the centre of which light is held still and time is said to stop, or not yet to have begun.

From a simple starting point, an innocent budding of the intellect, there may ensue a dogged, all-consuming undertaking which depletes the body, overstrains the senses and destroys the mind.

I can clearly recall the moment at which this interest in the names of the North Sea began. I was quickly scrolling through my library of images of historic maps—I believe it had to have been quickly, or else the effect would never have occurred—and as I did so the borderline of land and water as it made this sea on each map hopped and lurched in shape from one image to the next as if the sea were a living creature under the force of some paroxysm emerging from within itself. The name of this expanse of water, though, remained the same: there was a solidity—and a comfort in that solidity—to the wide-spaced placement of one letter after another across each blue expanse: NORTH SEA. The name, it is true, mutated in shape, position and size from one map to another, but still the sea was so much the North Sea that the words required no reading. But solidity, and comfort in solidity, is only understood when it is under threat of being taken away. Thus the ground was prepared for an aberration: on one of the maps the sea was denominated GERMAN OCEAN. It leapt off the screen in a shocking act of defamiliarisation. My initial assumption, that the conflict of the First World War must be responsible for the renaming—one, moreover, presented thus in the slender research into the matter—was quickly disproved by the most cursory glance at these maps' dates of production, the 'North Sea' being the denomination, I noted, on at least two mid-nineteenth-century maps.

And so it was that I began to collect these maps in earnest, and to look into their ways with names, to seek a story or a sense to the movement of time, which must be the same thing. I interrogated my database as if it were an ancient text which promised to disclose the greatest mysteries of the world, and returned to the maps, moving back step by step. Back I went, from Ernst Debes in 1876, through Bartholomew's Times maps of the 1860s, through the maps of Stielers, Peter-mann, Berghaus, back through Teesdale and maps made for Mitchell's School and Family Geography series, both in 1840, through Gilbert's in 1838 and Thomas Moule's the year before. Back I went, through John Cary's attractive presentation of 1811, through an anonymous map produced to commemorate the Franco-Russian treaties made at Tilsit in 1807, back through a 1749 Anglicised copy of Homann's Nuremberg production, whose representation of Britain and Ireland, with part of Holland, Flanders and France, it was pleased to describe as being 'agreeable to modern history'. Even in Thomas Bowles' plagiarised 1732 version of Herman Boll's original that expanse of water was denominated 'The British or North Sea' a full 150 years earlier than the academics describe the shift taking place. It was only upon reaching Robert Morden's maps of the first decades of the eighteenth century, published in Camden's Britannia, that the name change became observable. Morden's 1695 map designates it 'Germanicus Oceanus', while his 1722 map carries the legend 'The English or German Ocean'. Ten years later Bowles calls it 'The British or North Sea', and we arrive at the present habit for naming that watery mass.

Had I been capable of observing myself more clearly at that time, I might perhaps have found it reasonable to clear away all these maps, close the many dozens of tabs in my browser, shut my notebooks, to cease generating and turning over and through vast quantities of data as if they were those waters themselves. In fact, it would be true to say that within only a few hours I had gathered enough information to make a persuasive case, against the untenable argument of the academics, that it was the Hanoverian accession of 1714 rather than the war of two centuries later that was the cause of this alteration. Why, if I had my answer, then, did this task preoccupy me for many months further? This general truth—that the renaming of the North Sea was a grad- ual process tentatively initiated in reaction to the politics of the early eighteenth century—was not enough. It was not enough because it did not satisfy. I pursued this new interest as if I were a plant and it were the sun: relentlessly, somatically, and under the force of a desire which swept every other consideration into irrelevance. And so how could something so impoverished as an answer cause me to cease this undertaking? It could not.

Even as I worked, I knew that I drew further back from my aim—whatever that might have been. I extended and deepened my database of antique maps, read every article I could find on Anglo-German relations in the eighteenth and nineteenth centuries, studied the long cartographic tradition linking Britain and Germany, phoned leading researchers in maritime history at universities and research institutions all round the world, and yet the true and inner meaning behind this toponymic shift from 'German Ocean' to 'North Sea' drew further and further back from my view. It is only now that I can observe myself at that time and understand that the answer I was looking for, far from being the initial and particular spark of this alteration, was in fact the very recession of sense though these layers of information away from my comprehension. I had made of myself an engine of distraction.

When night came, I put away my work, ate a little if I remem- bered, and then took myself to bed, where I would lie down and surge through the dark waters of a now nameless mass, always down, down through the plaited currents, down into the motion- less fist-strong salted heaviness of it, down through the layers of sediment, marl, clay and rock, until, eventually, I found that cave which I had prepared without knowing for myself, one which the geology of the North Sea bed declares must be impossible—and yet here I am nevertheless—and in which, when lying there within its enclosure, I discovered there to be no necessity of sleep. A vast ocean of insomnia swelled up around me and I entered it willingly, with an avid hunger for that silent nightlong wakefulness which under normal circumstances would be intolerable.

Mike Silverton

Opera Poem

Opera isn't so much about what a hero, heroine or villain does
as in how he, she, it or they feel before, during and after an action.
When Phall learns that Vulv has departed via trebuchet to who knows where
his thoughts turn to rescue. However,
rather than dashing off as one would in what we call real life,
he steps forward and sings of his mad desire for vengeance.

Aria: "Away to autumn's bunting, mulchy, sodden Fate! Vulv outrages endures
as scene 'pon scene slips from view away, seven (7) clams remaining,
seven static, stoical clams."

Follow-up aria: "Tell me of Vulv one more time, again please."
It shows as only music can that Phall's love is genuine,
and that she, the diva, has given him her heart,
exclusive of aorta, liver slivers and dollops of spleen.

Stage left: Gypsies enter, feasting on acorns and rabbit debris,
quaffing grappa and bursting into waggish song,
"I shake your hand, now count your fingers."
And whilst our principal wonders aloud, "Could she be in this zany mob?"
his visage encounters a coconut-cream pie. What a funny indignity!
Interest shifts to fresh Gypsies hauling female acquisitions.
Ensemble: "This is your (our) dwelling now."

Where budgetary constraints apply, with top-shelf voices in short supply,
imagination's the thing. Imagine: Whilst milling about a bazaar,
Phall pauses to admonish a layabout. The lights dim, the layabout curses his fate.
This is opera. You're asked to believe.

For example, suppose a vermin loses incentive. Slinks away into its lair.
Just suppose. It costs you nothing. There is, as you've agreed to suppose, a beautiful queen—
princess really, possibly bogus—off at a distance. Behind a gauzy screen. Backlit. Weeping.
Her ladies in waiting cajole, plead, sing ditties, tall naughty jokes,
hop about with bright eyes flashing, getting nowhere.

48   EXACTING CLAM

As an event, a packaged entertainment, as tunes you hum as you leave the opera house,
a weeping queen is a simultaneity, a stylized occupation of time,
much like a portrait hovering midair.
Its fascination includes the likelihood of falling, damaging the elaborate frame.
Conversely, in opera, when we cannot see anything, much less hear it,
we fail to grasp its raisin debit. This failure to grasp an unheard event's raisin debit
might well be interpreted as a longing to embrace a metaphysical speculation.

The audience is adrift. One speaks of an ideal state.
The diva creates legends, topographical features even!
The diva is adrift. She recedes with the tide. She returns on a wave of expectation,
of wild carbonation!—the spirit of Schweppes or maybe spumante!
And so 'tis finally fixed, an unqualified abundance.

Meanwhile, a fop. Well, not exactly. Elsewhere puts it better.
A dandy. Homesick. Nostalgic. Drenched in sentimentality. Waterlogged.
The opera made it so. He recalls high teas, men's-room assignations,
the focus knob he fusses with, awaiting the diva.
His companions die. The cash in his billfold is no longer valid.
The heart he carved in the old oak tree a cardio-vascular network became.

Jim Meirose

Ten Liquids Barbering System— patendapendie

It's great to know exactly where to go when one needs to do something and. Yes, oh yes, I know, ole corporeal Father. I know I need to go to the barber. Its good to have a car to get there—see, nothing ought to be taken for granted as having a car to get someplace's who, 'er. Yes, I do need to go to the barber. Who 'ver 'em thinks thank you God for this so-handy car to get someplace like this, simple people. Yes, I really, really do. Don't thank God enough for the enough for the little things yak yak don't thank God don't enough thank God for the thank God enough, for the little things—let 'lone the barber eh—as a matter of fact most people go days 'n days before even thinking of God atoll, d'isla', at all's to let 'lone the barber that barbering-shop in that circular motion, yah, yo 'er thank heck for thank heck him for something for anything at anything at all ata all—b-h-h-h-her', we are, I am not, we we's wrong, I am juts, one man please, and thank you, hec heck he hec ho—okay parked right out front sorry in advance for not thanking you, God, aw, shucks heck a'tall anyway—thank you God, got some 'eadoh me-slelfe I did. Need to get to the barber I tell you. That's another reason a head-cut's in order. Gets to a point of order that one begins acting improperly 's a' sign a head-cut's in order; hence, we strode in this here barber-shop.

Thank God I got here.

I need to be here. I really do.

Whew.

Upsdidowndyslosh of an upended waterglass, how'd they do it?

Shut up, we just did. Don't slap God 'cross the face; if it's handed over, take it. Refuse not what your county can do to you; ask what you might do to your county. Think fast think fast who said that who did?

Ha, hah. Made you look!

Hic-syrup. Cheap in Los-Tanganiyeeka. Plough. The shop front was all bricked-in 'll 'cross. Eggs septum the doorway in. A doorway has to be provided to customers to enter if the shop's to be successful. Goes w'snot-sayyinne 'nnne—yes yes, and—this is the same place I remembered it. Right.

How to get here I meant. I mean. I do mean, I remembered, right, how to get here, all right. I moved to sit even though there was no one. Not wanting to look pushy, so what. Why 'o I need to explain each and every thing I do—well it just isn't right.

Having said that, my same old Sam Barber shook slight up his newspaper. As it brightly flamed over, he commented, There are so many things not right in the world. You know?

Uh-yeah.

Why, we are all not required to explain each and every thing we do. Ain't that right?

The paper he'd pulled that fact out from, well, assuming that was what he was talking about, as he've yet to speak out over it, go on, nod, act like the proverbial courtroom-lawyerindianne resonababble-up'd man.

Yas, s'pose. Seems right.

He swear—move still to go sit saying I am not rushing you I am much too down to rush about anything as if to out-trumpet with you, my body, I am above all and do not rush for none.

Okay, come on, says his shrug, please be seated, as eh yah but its okay if you are not ready as I rush for none thi' spasmodical fuse spasm'd-out usela' c-com on says yet another of the five allottable shrugs we require before final fuselage saying ok ah yeh if you fuse ins lage ist.

Airplanes!

Buzzzzzzz-z-zz—tumblededowning all apelike off'n tot the barberchair with the requisitized heavy scrolled ironical high polished footplate, and the flat black time-cracked cushiony airseat, and the likewise one on either side as you sit armrests, there is just one on either side what what why on earth would a hundred be needed, silly rabbit? Wasted in haste that would be uh! As a thousand chairbacks. Ten hundred priests.

Your hair will be cut in ten evenly spaced discrete portions. Are you ready to proceed?

Ready to proceed's uh uh yes tee-indicationed qiout clearly and well by the seating you see now before you, sir.

Yah sure.

Good. Say the manner or style to be achieved.

Oh sure. No problem 'cause every workman wants his product to be of benefit now, was—uck uh tell into the mirror thrust up the wall, somehow solidly cemented in with the barber to the light side, turned off slightly exactly, precisely, from what he has come to expect, short, of course. Just short—to ask more is beneath 's as fashion-sylisticing's 'yond blow us. So what right 'n ready. The head-cutter's not got entirely what h' or s'plug in the correct pre—'he needs.

Yes.

Sooess preparitations 'rer proceeds there's time for one quickly casual but fast enough to fit the probable time available overscan 'f the already overscanned once per visit but as the visits've been quite farhuff hip-hearted, the memories are dim, being a flesh and blood creature with all the typical flaws and failings built in as appendices to these wholes calculated by our supreme creator after the fall. Hiss. I am afraid many reams of card stock will be needed for this one. The head-cut the head-cut and the strang' fuselage to the right's sound that is indeed

a wonderful tightly wound word and as what's severed to the Wright's brother perhaps flying in from what's right up left atop the high cabinet's the same musty slick ol' Napoleon with his hand like he does with her mooning left and her sister smiling right and some kind of ad man's copywords scrolled upsides someplace it's been there for ages, regarding some long discontinued hair-root rejuvinizalling lotion. Hiissss. Yes ages. Hiii-issssssss. Dostoyotricksky's said ages before the consummation of his life's   m o s t frightening lie.

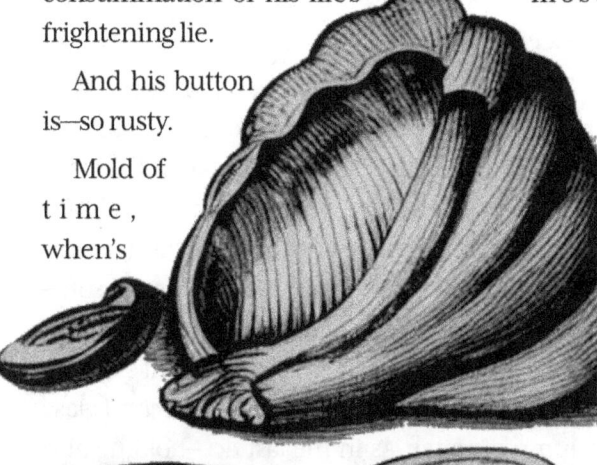

And his button is—so rusty.

Mold of t i m e , when's

the last time he touched, makes sense to wonder that of the barberbutt not of you s'cause to touch that you'd get edjecteid as it is not yours to touch it. But. Los! By Tom Poston's ghost, look right—a liquid barbery tall'd inverted glass of water 'pside down glassa-wattah how'd they get it that way but its holding large blackout buzz clippers and they pull the up pull up the glass how can a great column of water stand like it's a new element three atoms uptop their other with a superfast half-life est' will not defeat gravity, my headtop's liquid-barbered all 'cross as the column slumps into it-self, spreads very grey, very wet, as the concrete mix's slump test off'n the new batch by a knowl-edgeable mixer technician before the mixertruck can travel to the elemental sub-basement initial exciting first day of new construction's site. The liquid barber's a sheen 'cross the floor and the headtop's now cut to perfection and it must have been done by this fascinating new technology only read of noplace at all up 'til now.

Geez!

The top's perfect and so fine a shop is this that there's has not been a need to judge the quality of the job for so long, so on this day, it's a lie to say yes, the cut looks good, because that can't be said honestly without close critical inspection, and if that's not done—no matter what's the reason—then expressing any judgement of the quality of the work is a lie, or at the least downright sloppy—here a rattle and tap 'gain out right a second glass column of water. As in the last act—holding also maybe the same set of buzzy-nippers and the glass' pulled up and rip rap left right down and up 'midst flying fine clipping-mist the right side's, well, its done and the water clugg-spread out into a merge with th sheen of the first liquid and how many more are needed to complete this whole job since they only p' u' up must say at this point, we're all placidly domingoed. And the workmen work heavily brooming the flood out the back loading dock doors. And so the human in control casually spoke there seems to be multi-ple weather reports predicting ice-cold rain. That but? Brrrrrrrrrrrrrr, I say. You?

Ah yes. Brrrrrrrrrrrrrrrrrrrrrrrrrrrrrrrrrrrrrrrr-r-rrrr—me too.

A fine day otherwise. You enjoy a fine day as I do?

Hok! Who wouldn't?

Yay, noke. Nop', no one. Ready for a next? Pos-sibly the back? Or do you want to freshen up f-wrist? There's a washroom in your back, see the door—oh no, silly me! How could that be, Menzar-role? Eyes not popped up your back-head, Willy? You of the divisional meeting Yarley'd out 'er 'ck? So rattlin'-taptical is this attitude of yours. Jeeez! F'you were here I would actually tell you! Silly me. Silly me.

Proper politics.

Silly me.

Yes, literally.

Procreatable Ben. And procreatable Billy. You read of that scandal up in town?

Yes!

Some few banners got flown then, of re-sisquishable smalltalk, before the next twelve-foot tall glassbounded inverted by magic liquid fast-barber appeared. Stepping up—pull! And then my some by this time irritably applied magic the curved-back o' mah head guts shaved down. Old smokey! You said do it short. Read that in the paper? If they put it in the paper, well—it must be donut-true. The president's always the smartest man in the country—write that down Ole' Coloned-up Lon Taleho. He of old-schooly warehousing and dry humor fame. Unfortu-nately now in the cemetery. The best carvings are under the seats up those back catheterlidrical kneel-up, 'n down,'n pray, pews. Witness to his glory! Do ye believe, Tipper? State if ye believe!

Ah sure. Sure as gowns. Shatter-blasted B-bar-ber hit by car shattering three hundred sixty de-gree water blood shower, luminol, luminol; lu-minoolleeeeeeeeeeeeeeeeeeeee-e-e—e-eeeeee---e---0-ee3-e---gasssssssssssssssss-s-s---s----ss. Y'know?

Aw surely. Rot. But, anyway.

The 'ee must have been getting pressured by the entry of a short column of customers filed in, flipp'd hats up precisionly hung, then got seated. As they grasped confusedly at the spare spread of unusual, seldom seen, and when seen usually months o'data-date, simultranistingly came they at my sides two tall inverted wide fluter'd versions of the common water glass, but just timesed up by twelve, possibly—these went to work much as their prior similaritarians had, pulled up faster than flash, and as the columns of water instantly fell in on themselves, three simultaneously, mind you—each slashed its final instant into—and get this—three thirteenths or thus as far as could be captured, comb hold snip snap thirteen and twelve; comb hold snip snap eleven ten and half the-th' nine; comb hold snip snap the rest of the nine plus the eight and the seven, and, comb hold snip snap six five four two three one—and fifteen it seemed, though probably just one made fast by the threat of losing his job if they didn't immediately shoot out from backstage brooming out broom sloshing waved out before them broom-pushing brooming out the three's worth of lifeless water out the front o' the door, but not before tossing back the three combs three clippers into the seemingly bass-mouthed gulp of a well-tarnished autoclave back ot' the side space; quick as if setting up for a double stake-burnin' in Hot Town's centralized village squarespace tonight. Dead space in the room over a huge snowy-blowlersettled super-orange gleam of a machine always set there fur is s'long as that cat run off there probably remembered; the final wow of this whole bean being, each comb and clipper was thoroughly inspected for cracks lumps bruises or black eyes before and all this all this at once at once together hot cubed like just one more component took for granted as a magic black box cloud as a whisper which would have formerly required ten dozen squads of high-drained energy-nears 'r some fars also—to accomplish the same and in twenty times less of a saving of time as is done here and now in this very

today! And being so astonished yet, the hump-barber just now slid out of a long thin simultaneous banter 'bout this days moon launch, them Yankees, and that other tragedy over there. Thank God it's his summer.

After all this tiny bump does the work formerly requiring scores of vacuum tubes, miles of wiring, and several acres of floorspace.

Now ain't that sump'im?

Oooo, yah—sa' as he stepped left, leany-peering at the steady line of haircuts to do filing in taking seats, it was amazing that—each and every one's hefting a big newsflap before him—the amazing being that there were none there when I came. And also being that even though nearly fifty-five clients set now steadily reading, there are more papers on the paper by the minute, no doubt supplied as all is supplied no doubt, no doubt supplied by the very lord the son of his father the master of all creation so spit, p'shaw, hey—what's making a few extra papers matter given those calculations. By great thunder and now the finaliteen cutters take the stage, but.

But.

Elderly ladies hair now and again sink with lean-back half moon halfling'o a fat la-lunette, like drenched the one time at a fancy never go again shop me got forced into for the lack of this here place right now. Hip! The old woman came in and the female hairbob came from the back and the old woman began to get her treatment, for, hap-parently 's i' a full-svc shop by golly me and I bet as I got so drenched com com par-ey, huh, best not to pay tension as the lasts are now here to finish off me. Better concentrate. Better concentrate.

Better hard-concentrate right about now. Will look so good 'll need to go find a job to interview into.

So I told her, I'm having a really hard time reading this score. How the hell can I play it properly this way? Huh? Huh? Huh? Huh? I am a su-pertip't back bright lounge of a singer, after all—b-b-b-b-b-b-b-b-bbbbut right here the world ended.

Sorry.

<blankness> ay oh no just joking you I love the occasional inappro-priate joke, mastamatta' oof fact so do every chaired down butt here waiting in the shop loves to laugh inappropriately do it good. And do it often and by that Huck Finney no the world of course has not ended at least not over here but you are over there and with-out being over there I can't judge of over there's still here after all my span of experience's only fine tuned to know what the hells going on over here not over there plus after all with these five tall watered-down strangers comb-ing and clipping combing clipping and laughing a falling their water down out and merged with each one's each others how can I hell the know that what's side going in out over there mah-mah patooey!

Slap-dat-'dere herd of, eh, what—let me see—didn't bring my glasses along today hot damn well I'll be of course I already am that was stupid—yes, it is, a herd of big hippos. Not just any herd of hippos, getcha-t' understand—but a herd of big hippos. Yes. Really really big hippos. Huge hippos.

Cartageneically? Yes, of course, this model may be used cartageneically but beware—which means really careful—models later than this, which, although bearing the Big Boss Boy label, are of much over quality since those buddies in their fast flamed up GTX cars sucked up a hairs more than three-fourths of the remaining com-mon stock. The rest's well known—b' hey.

The grannymam backed in the porcelain half lunetted out drainsink must be done w' 'er 'sh a' th' young 'ady wheeling her out in her gunrack over to the seldom used, and when used most often improperly installed, extra black barber chair mot hip think is never h'p used h' i' p' at all—she passed my back unseen draped round with a headtowel Easter Is-land topknot style much too wide for her and heavy for her, her neck! My neck! God, I think they have broken my neck! This can-not be my last swim! Please do not tell me that! Tell me there is hope, doctor! There must there must be hope there hope there must be.

Yep. But yes—what dad? Yes I knew I needed to go to the barber. Why the hell else would I be here dad?

F'huh?

When the laughter subsided, Bud himself came out brushing blonde bristles all round my neck—aren't they nice—to head off the after-cut itching. The itching that rises slowly from a slight awareness about half the drive home to a flaming need for immediate relief causing massive bolts to the inadequately staffed shower strip down even when not there yet strip down yes haste will be necessary—so be grateful for the brush—but Bud himself turn't to just one last waterslump to be brushed out the gate and, at last glance really waking, all stepped back saying rise—rise—rise—rise 'n stepcross the room.

By all that's big Freedomland—looks good if all do say it themselves.

Isn't it great to know exactly where to go when one needs to do something and? Do you believe me now son, by my lord, do you believe me now?

Ca-ching.

No, no—keep the change.

Terese Svoboda

Three Poems

Rancher Vision

Among the cows I slaughtered:
  long-lashed and horned
            as thick-furred as yaks
               the big eyes blinded by
weed-scratch

            Meat takes down the planet
but I can't see it
  for the floaters and flashers
and

a man be-gouled by lipstick
  hungry
  beside a Subway bag

IF YOU SEE SOMETHING

The climate does not see me
  nor the cows eating eating eating
their deaths   not to mention
                           methane belched

        the planet rocking
me chewing

It's as if I wince
  so someone else sees it:

who stood there with the hammer

Tilt Windmills

The sky tilts as in a bad book, *Revelations:*
the apocalypse, a too-many syllabled end.

It's a calypso really, the sky tilts to St. Lucia,
the dance you all think you've been doing

—not just me—the scent of sea almonds
strictly strychnine underfoot. The sky tilts

as in a casino and all the cash pours out,
a cloudburst, a weeping of your want.

Are you so sure of your want? The taxes alone,
the new friends. The sky tilts and you fall,

the vertigo James Stewart's, the view a bird
who's used to it. Winged others pick you up—

stewardesses? Assume the position, upright citizen.
Who's on that donkey making jokes?

Peanuts

Let the bag of peanuts rain upon your window—
it's elephantine, the way quarantine hungers

for useless gesture. I've not washed these evil hands
and they steal to each orifice, proving

nothing's guilty except Darwin's impulses:
the virus must live and slough in swarm

to the floor, its elegant purple spikes trammelled
or not, its Otherness not subject to the foot

but ether remade to lethal.
Thus worship with downward dog

and know your neighbors harbor hands
like yours, and that windows will fly open.

Randy Prunty

Letters Written Upon Awakening

Dear Skelly

We knew the stick
was a branch
on which fruit might hang. My

oh my
what a wonderful bird
in polyphony
the frogs are.

Dear Man at the Gate

Thank you for
that something thing
I can't remember
that saved me.

I hate to die in dreams. I'm

getting out of bed now
as you suggested
using my foot
as a bookmark.

Dear Ancestor

I tried to get your trick.
How you said your name
is the act: *Persona Oscura*
continuously

setting the table
then whisking away the tablecloth
to reveal your face
as phonemes
scarred into the wood.

Dear Bucky Fuller

Teacher, I made a geodesic dome
from pool noodles.

You know I'm special. Why

are you testing me?

Dear Mindy Dawn Friedman

Trying yet again
to go back to college. No

amount of advice
could top your oracular empathy:
"You don't need to water the grass when it's raining."

Safe Word

Jenny foraged in the refrigerator snatching chocolate cake and Yoo-hoo, placing it on the counter, and pecking at it hunched over like a vulture, while ignoring her mother sitting at the kitchen island. It was lockdown Wednesday in the school district and all three of the kids looked forward to the shooter drills with muted excitement. Jenny wore her neon bull's-eye t-shirt. Todd went full head-to-toe camo with green, black, and tan paint streaked across his face and neck. Ben dressed as a smaller version of Todd, but his camo outfit and face paint reflected the Hello Kitty tones of pink, magenta and grey.

"This is the first time freshman get to compete for the role of crazed shooter." Todd poked the toaster with a steak knife. His strawberry strudel disintegrated deep in the innards of the toaster and refused to come out. "I can't wait to hunt down and shoot Missy bull's-eye here." He pointed at Jenny with his knife dripping strawberry ooze.

Marge chose not to comment on Jenny's breakfast choices, repeating her mantra, "Pick your battles." The mantra had been imposed on her by her husband who constantly scolded her for picking fights with the kids. Marge calmly told Jenny she didn't agree with her fashion choices. "I think it sends the wrong message."

"Why do you hate me so much?" Jenny hissed.

"It just looks like you're asking for it," Marge said.

"What's the big deal Marge? No one else cares if their kids wear bull's-eyes to school," Jenny said.

Which battles to pick? It didn't matter whether she chose to fight or walk away, she felt deeply wounded whenever she talked to her teenagers. "Watch your tone."

Jenny made a snarky face and stuck her tongue at Marge.

Codi, Jenny's best friend, appeared out of nowhere and made a peanut butter and marsh-mallow sandwich for her breakfast. Marge suspected she was secretly living in their basement but anytime she broached the subject with Jenny, it led to a huge screaming match, which ended with her husband telling Marge to pick her battles.

"Todd, look at this." Codi peeled open her coat to reveal a purple Kevlar vest with a nervously painted bull's-eye in black and white. "Isn't this cool?" She didn't want to get overheated with all the running and screaming so she chose not to wear a shirt. Jenny and Todd agreed that she was a genius.

Bulletproof vests had become mandatory school dress code ever since Ms. Willow the English teacher mistook a surprise lockdown drill for real. In self-defense she had to shoot two cops and three students. The "accidental" shooting of Mr. Deener, the shop teacher, was still under investigation. Some believed the bullet in Mr. Deener's butt was personal having more to do with an illicit affair gone bad than self-defense.

"Todd, Jenny's going to do my makeup. Should I put a bullet hole in my neck or forehead," Codi giggled.

Marge couldn't tell if Codi had a crush on Todd or Jenny or both.

"Why decide? Why not both?" Marge said.

"Great idea, Mom," Codi said. Codi was the only one to call the Gundersons Mom and Dad even though she wasn't related.

"Yeah, great," she called after the girls as they rushed off. The only time anyone took Marge seriously was when she was joking. She decided to pick her battles and not say anything.

Marge continued digging something out of the barrel of a Hello Kitty BB gun with a fork. "Were you trying to shoot gummy bears?" She said to Ben, her six-year-old. "How sweet."

"No. I ran out of pellets," Ben said.

"Don't you think the world would be a happier place if guns shot gummy bears instead of bullets?"

The boys groaned and rolled their eyes. She expected that from the older one, but Ben? Marge had thought there was still time before Ben deemed her stupid and meaningless.

Todd stopped eating his Cookie Crunch cereal mid slurp, "Meow bang bang."

Ben screamed, "Marrrrggge. Todd's teasing me again." He buried his face in Marge's lap and sobbed. Marge petted his long uncombed hair and absorbed all the affection she could from the only child who still needed her.

Marge gave Todd a serious cut-it-out look. In an overly loud voice she said, "We have worked very hard to help Ben understand that there is nothing wrong with boys loving Hello Kitty."

The girls returned to the kitchen to show off Jenny's copper bullet earrings and their makeup. Jenny sported a red circle blended with black on her temple with the red bleeding down her face and neck. The girls said it was the latest style.

"Look Mrs. Gunderson," Codi revealed a shaved spot in her sandy blonde hair. Marge gagged at the festering red and black wound. The hair surrounding the make-believe wound was mangled with green goo. "We decided to make a third bullet hole. Everybody at school is going to be jealous." Codi gave Jenny a groping hug. "Thanks Jen."

"Is the makeup necessary?" Marge said, deciding half way through her question that this wasn't a battle worth fighting. Marge grabbed a toaster pastry and dunked it in her coffee.

Ben scooted next to Todd at the kitchen island hugging his Hello Kitty BB gun and slurped his rocky road yogurt topped with jimmies. They paged through *Gun Life* squealing at all the flashy colors and cool features of the new AK-47 models.

"We need to make it as realistic as possible, *Marge*. Otherwise the kids won't take safety seriously." Jenny's habit of calling her Marge mixed with her stop-talking-to-me-you-stupid-idiot tone left Marge gasping for air. Her laid-back husband insisted she not take it personally. '*They're teenagers*' he'd say as if that were a panacea. She couldn't help but feel the shrapnel of every sharp word embedded in her skin, gut, chest, foot. She ached all over.

"In my day," Todd mocked his mother using a shaky granny voice, "school was a safe place except for all those dinosaurs stomping around and eating the slow ones."

Jenny defended her brother insisting they were learning important life skills.

"I'm concerned these drills will traumatize you kids," Marge said.

"Haven't you ever heard 'What doesn't kill, maim, or emotionally cripple us makes us stronger?'" Todd said.

"Yeah, Mom. Don't you want us to be strong?" Codie physically inserted herself into the middle of the conversation.

"You don't get it, Marge. Trauma is the new black." Jenny spoke with the drama of a beat poet. "Trauma creates the high notes in the dull drudgery of life. Trauma is life!"

"In my day, we never had metal detectors, lockdown drills, or fear," Todd spoke in his shaky granny voice. "We had to walk to school in twenty feet of snow without shoes, pants, or bras in the middle of the summer."

They laughed at Marge's old fashioned ignorance.

"OMG. What about sound effects?" Jenny grabbed Cody's arm. They glared into each other's eyes, sharing the same thought.

"Like bang, bang, bang?" Marge said.

"No, Marge." Jenny rolled her eyes.

"Oh, thank God," Marge said.

"Rapid machine gun fire..." Codi said and then Jenny finished her thought, "with our screaming dubbed over the gun noise . . ." Codi finished their thought, now holding both of Jenny's arms, "recorded on our phones." They jumped up and down with excitement.

Marge choked out the words "Do you really think . . ." and then loudly blurted, "that's a good idea?" Marge strained to keep a neutral expression for fear of being ostracized for her out-of-touchness.

Jenny only heard part of Marge's question and squeezed her with enthusiastic warmth. "Thanks for the praise, Marge."

Realizing she'd lost this battle, Marge relaxed and sopped up the insincere affection.

"That's stupid," Todd said. "You'll be screaming your heads off running away from me as the fake shooter."

Jenny flicked Marge away. "You're stupid," she said to Todd. "What if we've been shot? We won't be able to scream then."

Codi draped her arm around Jenny's shoulders. "Yea, what if we're dead?"

Ben chewed the heads off three gummy bears sticking out of barrel of the BB gun.

"Oh, that makes a lot of sense." Todd mocked the girls letting his vowels drop deep into his throat. "If you're dead, how can you push the play button?"

"We won't be dead, because you'll never be picked to play the role of crazed shooter." Jenny said.

Codi stuck her tongue at Todd.

"STOP fighting!" Marge said.

"What's the big deal?" Ben said with red-stained lips.

Ron Gunderson came limping down the stairs. He'd injured his big toe during a handgun safety check. He insisted they needed a gun to keep the family safe. Marge's cat was collateral damage in that whole fiasco but dare Marge mention one more time that Ron should have checked the gun for bullets—that according to Ron was fighting words.

"Why do you always pick a fight with the kids before school?" Ron said to Marge. "Why can't we eat breakfast in peace?"

"It wasn't me," Marge said.

They all laughed at her.

Ron shook his head. "You need to choose your battles, honey."

Marge turned red. "Jenny and Todd started it."

"That's so random, Marge," Todd said.

Ron exchanged a look with the kids that signaled everyone should shut up and let Marge think she was right.

"How is you toe feeling, honey?" Marge said.

Ron's half lidded eyes and pursed lips was his way of saying he didn't appreciate her passive aggressive comment.

Todd looked at his cell phone. "Sweet. The cafeteria is serving liver, cauliflower brains, and ketchup for lunch."

"I love their lockdown cupcakes," Codi said. "They make 'em with raspberry sauce bleeding from a candy bullet puncturing the flesh colored icing."

Ron gave the kids another look, which meant that it was time to leave for school. They collected their backpacks and headed for the door.

Marge gave Jenny, Todd, and Ben a bear hug. Codi weaseled her way into the middle of the pack. Marge buried her nose into Ben's hair and instructed them to be safe.

Jenny wrestled away from her mother's suffocating arms. "God Marge, you act like it's a big deal if I never come home."

"It's just a fact of life, Marge," Todd said. "One or all three of us will be gunned down at school one of these days,"

Codi raised her finger indicating that she wanted to be included in the body count.

"It's the price we pay for a free education. So, chill. It's no big deal," Todd said.

"Yeah, this is America where we have the freedom to live and die as we choose," Jenny said.

"She's got a point," Ron said.

"I plan on dying in the process of living, not locked up in your paranoid schizophrenic boredom capsule." Todd kissed his mother on the cheek. "Ron, tell Marge to strap on her Beretta Nano and go out and live a little."

"Yeah Marge, you can't keep us boarded up in this boring 'safe' house for the rest of our lives," Jenny said. "Safe. Like that's a real thing. Doh is it even a word?"

Three Poems From "Prayers in the Evacuation Garden"

"Hollyhock"

Forgive me, but
I play with words

When I learned
Your blessed name

I teetered on the edge
Of an obscenity

"Holy cock," you see
Is what came to mind

But *"No such thing*
As a holy cock"

Even the Bible notes
Spirit, not flesh,

Visited the Virgin Mary
To birth Baby Jesus

The encyclopedia harrumphs
At me, pinches my cheekiness

And lectures that your name
Goes back to an early saint

Everything about your name
Is *blessed, blessed, blessed*

Derived from Middle English
"Holi"—so what's with my cheek?

Nothing or all is sacred to me—
I am a poet, thus, remind you

of these flowers' mythology: crusaders
Brought them to Europe from

The "Holy Land" where they
Grew in abundance. Yet another

Theft arising from a larger story
Of men waging war for false gods

As it turns out, the myth is false
But it says everything about Humanity

Including how mere rhyme surfaces
A lie, simply for immediate gratification

Kindness, And Its Ease

The sunflowers look
naked. We did not choose
them, these "volunteer"
plants that rose amidst
a modest corn field
we planted to experiment.
But the corn was uprooted
to prepare for a new year,
leaving sunflowers tall under
a summer moon's spotlight
and missing their skirts.
The sand-colored corn
husks were rough, not lace,
velvet, linen or cashmere.
But they sufficed to
distract from their skinny,
bowed legs. Now, they
must depend on their faces,
tanned to leather from
looking straight at the sun

and still discernible despite
their yellow bonnets.
"But we're not roses,
zinnias or hollyhocks.
We're not lovely."
Such silliness, I sigh.
I won't lie—I do not care
for sunflowers. But,
today, they shall grace
a spectacular crystal vase.

Nerium Oleander, Shorter Than Kerima

You are as gigantic as a megalodon
whose mouth looms over the sky that fell
into my landlord's swimming pool

You hosted a baby heron that ate its sibling
But, still, I admired you from the distance
of standing beneath your flowers—

braggadocious clusters of blooms
radiating whites, pinks and reds
easily holding up the non-fallen sky

I did not know you grew poison
until this cold morning when I fell to my knees
beating this ground, hardened by drought

unlike the other side of the planet
where land remains damp from water
which, recent science proves, retains memory

But I did not know your beauty
masks poison that would destroy
my family if they thought to caress you

Stunned, I learned even the smallest fragment
from your thin petals can send my dogs
to join you, **Kerima Lorena Tariman**

killed by the Armed Forces' 79th Infantry
Battalion in Silay City, Negros Occidental
on August 20, 2021—the evening before

the 38th anniversary of the assassination
of Benigno Aquino, Jr., sparking other People's
Revolutions around the world. I hammered

the ground with tight fists bleeding
a color that belongs among your blossoms
mourning the flower prematurely destroyed

A flower's biological function is to facilitate
reproduction through pollination, causing
its ovary to develop into fruit containing seeds

Then I smelled the blood we share, its
conflicted rust lifting me to stand and look back
at you, a shrub as charismatic and amoral

as too many politicians—but you are not the only
creature hardy enough to survive being hacked
down, leveled to unfamiliar ground

Kerima's flower shall be generous with seeds
blossoming to grow a Homeland no longer
Imaginary, no longer abstracted by corruption

We are a people as hardy as you and, soon
our Motherland shall be watered by other
sources than the veins of sacrificed poets

Nick Holdstock

Witness

I f asked, the cows would tell the police of a light that smeared the dark. They would say it moved at head height (theirs, not humans) as it moved down towards the woods.

Those trees would complain. The young man snapped their slender limbs as he hurried through. He was inconsiderate, in too much of a hurry. His tears were no excuse.

The stream known as 'Tumbling Bay' did not engage with him. As soon as his foot entered the water it quickly moved aside. This was nothing personal, it had so much to do, always somewhere else to be.

'Even as a kid, Steve was a little shit. He was always hanging around the farms but didn't want to help. Whenever he saw someone smoking he'd try to ponce one. Once he took another kid's bike, then went off with it for two days. When he got caught he said he'd just borrowed it.'

Steve made a greater impression on the bank. He gouged it when he slipped; he clawed it as he fell. But unlike the trees the mud did not resent this damage. It had learned to accept that sometimes people left a trace of their passing.

From its high vantage the owl regarded Steve. The human's pulse was fast, but whether this was from excitement or fear, the owl had no idea. It had other concerns. Beneath the human's noise it could hear the fluttering heart of a vole.

'And even though Steve kept trying to smoke he made a really big deal of his asthma. He was always puffing on his inhaler or waving it around. It was in his mouth so often it was like a baby's dummy. My mate who works in a hospital says a lot of kids have asthma because they want attention.'

Steve squelched into the field, then stopped. The ground felt his weight shift as he leaned forward, then back onto his heels, his feet transmitting agitation, purpose, yet remaining in place. They seemed to have a destination but not the will to travel.

'Not that Steve got much attention. His mother was already off with some bloke in Wales and his dad was drunk most of the time. The only person who really cared was his uncle, and look at the thanks he's got. They made a right funny pair. Adam must be six-one and you can tell he goes to the gym. A lot of them do. But even after puberty Steve was short and pasty. He looked like he had a cold all the time, he was always wiping his nose with his hand, then rubbing it on his sleeve. He was disgusting.'

Water was lodged in the old wood of the stile, so although the wood knew Steve's hand it could not remember when they had met before. It could only recall that this hand been accompanied by a larger one, a hand with a firmer grip.

'Most weekends the two of them went off swimming or cycling. For an asthmatic kid Steve was pretty active. When he was with Adam he was like a different boy. Every time I saw them together Steve was laughing. Adam couldn't have done more for Steve. His plate was really full. He had his job in Hastings and his own parents to take care of and apparently a boyfriend in Battle. I never saw him but my sister saw the two of them holding hands at the end of the station platform. She said that from a distance the bloke was a bit older, maybe forty, also very good looking.'

A fox watched from the brambles. As the steps came nearer it tensed. When the thing appeared it relaxed. The thing was moving sluggishly, as if wounded. This thing was no threat.

Over the woods, the fields, the lane, the bloated raincloud hung. It alone could see the top of Steve's head. But despite its privileged position, it could not see through his skull. Thoughts were not like weather. Neither his headlong descent into the woods, or his stumbling progress through the fields, could have been used to make a forecast. There was absolutely no way for a cloud to know Steve's intentions.

'But although Adam did all that for Steve, it wasn't enough. Just after he was sixteen there were a stormy few weeks when he was trying to get Adam to let him move into his caravan. It was a massive place, with three rooms, but still, a caravan. Of course Adam said no. He was an adult who had his own life. But Steve wouldn't take no for an answer. People saw him crying and making a fuss. It was pathetic.'

Steve's reflection moved across the windows of the Oak Tree Inn. The pub could have told him Adam wasn't inside. It could have said his uncle hadn't been there for six months, and because it was an old pub—est. 1685—that had seen and heard most things, that his uncle wasn't likely to be there ever again. But why would it have said anything? It was hard enough to keep a village pub going without getting involved in that kind of mess.

'So you could say he's always loved drama. And over the last six months he's put on a real show. It's been like watching one of those reality programmes except he's put the whole village in it too. Bloody journalists. If they'd tried to interview me, I'd have told them where to go.'

Soft, regular sounds whose volume increased and then the figure came into view. He was seen, smelt, and then there was a new noise that sometimes killed. It approached quickly, rushed to attack and then there was a moment of blindness. When the figure took two steps into the wood the badger moved away.

'I can see why Steve's Dad was sceptical. He didn't want to believe it, and I suppose I can't blame him. Poor old Dave was already in a bad way, what with his wife off in Wales and his liver packing up. The last thing he needed was his son accusing his little brother of abusing him. Dave didn't say anything to anyone for two weeks, and it must have been awful for him because he thought the

world of Adam. And when Dave told me what Steve had said, I admit I had my doubts as well.'

The taillights saw a reddened figure emerge from the gateway, walk ten paces, then bend to the ditch. The car had been to a film where another man in the woods in a red light was digging and digging then threw another man into a hole. Something was not right but as ever the problem was that the car was moving away. Nothing could be done. The last they saw he was straightening while holding a large object that resembled one it possessed.

'And if there was ever a boy who was going to cry wolf. Even while Steve was telling me about when him and Adam got soaked and had to take off their clothes in the caravan, I was thinking he was probably making it up. If it had been now, when Steve's 18, I wouldn't have done anything. But Steve wasn't an adult then, and although I didn't like him, I knew what was right. If a kid says something like that, you have to act like you believe them, even when you don't.'

From the branch of an elm a pheasant heard the chain on the jerrycan knock against the metal. But this noise meant nothing to the bird. Its functional and fortunate brain couldn't associate that sound with anything. It had never heard the ticking of a gas fire turned up to full, the ache of metal expanding with heat. The pheasant's life was hard and rarely satisfying: it was usually either hungry or frightened. But it always knew what it wanted.

The only human who saw Steve that night was Gavin in the village hall. Gavin was alone in the dark, in a bubble of silence, breathing in as much quiet and calm as any mollusc could. Of course Gavin was not a clam or oyster or any kind of bivalve. He was a 57 year-old-man who knew his wife was cheating on him again.

'So I took Steve down to the police station. I went in with him and thought I'd have to wait a bit but I was there for three hours. I didn't want to get involved but they had a lot of questions and I couldn't not answer them. I had to be honest. I had to tell the police about when Steve kept crying. I had to tell them about when I saw Adam and those two gypsy boys messing about by the river. They were all wet and laughing. They were almost naked.'

The jerry can was tired of being scraped along the road. The hand holding it didn't seem to know whether to hold on or let go. And so the pheasant, fox and badger heard its scraped protest. They heard and thought it was terrible but they had not asked to hear that sound. Hearing did not oblige them to help.

'And I'm not stupid. I know they're not the same. I like young women, but that doesn't mean I want to fuck little girls.'

One of the surveillance cameras saw Steve approach the caravan. He was moving slowly, often stopping to rest. Once he came closer the camera saw he was crying. He put the jerry can down, then walked out of the frame. The camera watched the jerry can do nothing. There was the usual branches, the road. Then, after twenty-eight seconds, the camera saw him return and pick up the can.

   Another camera saw Steve unscrew the cap and then tilt it so tentatively he could have been watering flowers. He poured petrol on the deck chairs, then around the caravan. He was shaking and his lips were moving but what he said was not heard.

'All the same, it can happen. It does happen. After Adam got arrested a lot of people said they'd always thought he was dodgy. But that was bollocks. Up until then they were all really proud of themselves for not minding that a gay bloke was living in the village. Bloody two-faced gits. By the time Adam appeared in court they were calling him a monster. And so when he said Steve was the one who'd tried it on with him, and he'd said no, nobody believed him.'

Two green woodpeckers were woken by the acrid smell. It was harsh, and yet compelling. They wanted to never smell it again. They wanted to get closer.

In the caravan Adam's cat was half-asleep on her cushion while watching her human twitch. She thought he was calmer. He'd swallowed blue things.

'I didn't know what to believe. I'd done my duty but I was just trying to stay out of it. Though one thing I do know is that it's weird for an adult to be living in a caravan. No one who's normal does that. But Adam's lawyer did a real number on Steve. He kept contradicting himself. And although I've had my problems with the law, I know that if a court says someone's not guilty you have to leave it at that. Believe what you want, it's a free country, but you have to accept a verdict.'

The petrol was almost-fire. Flame followed so logically, so naturally, it was surely inevitable. Yet there was disbelief. It had been incomplete for as long as it could remember. Sloshing in darkness, hearing echoes. Now it was free, out in the open; surely it and oxygen could join.

'I mean, what's the alternative? We can't have people getting lynched because a weird kid makes things up. Those blokes who smashed up Adam's caravan were bang out of order. Even if you don't like gays, that's going too far.'

Steve's clothes were already wet but they made a good effort. Petrol tasted new and strange but they did not complain. They drank until they were full.

   Hands were holding the lighter but they weren't really his. Those fingers did whatever they wanted, they touched and they pointed. Even now, after the verdict, they still believed they might succeed in gaining Adam's fingers. It wasn't impossible. They loved that doubt.

   But fire was certainty.

Rodrigo Toscano

Two Poems

Sentinels

Fractalled feathers
    of Whitman's wings
        croon on
about 'American'
    what it means
        what it might
varieties of fruits
    for some reason
        get play there
more often birds
    and these days
        butterflies abound
Alongside this scene
    expect a 'father'
        long lost (found)
at every strophe
    expect a 'mother'
        tongue forking
(what's that word?
    few know it
        less care)
Then *personal* habits
    baldly revealed
        to recloak
State department
    payroll cousin
        also a finalist
something about clouds
    making faces
        at grandma
a pomegranate
    drops from the sky
        splatters
'seeds are silent tears
    of past deeds'
        finger snaps
'because you see—'
    <transcendence cadence>
        finger snaps
Lab coat level clean
    while mining
        and caching
Lab coat level clean
    while *throttling*

        the competition
Fractalled eyeballs
    of Whitman's eaglets
        squawk on
of becoming 'whole'
    another sovereign
        among sovereigns
Varieties of gramps
    perching on ginkgos
        on standby
Sooner than later
    the rhombus haircut
        or newfound scar
By nomination only
    iron butterflies
        finger snaps

Cuddlers

"What do we want!?
    incremental change!
When do we want it!?
    in due time!"

Thus, the hatchback of
    relative comfort
down-dogs
    into position

From this precision
    the heirs
are craftily
    'anti-capitalist'

"What do we want!?
    safe aspirations!
When do we want it!?
    when they yield!"

Thus, the garage door of
    alibi storage
seals shut
    the shame shimmy

"What do we want!?
    poet Lagoon Valdez!
Why do we want him!?
    he's cuddly"

Ian Boulton

previously / currently / shortly

previously

1. People like me and you do not get by on instinct. We are as unlikely to say 'I just had a gut feeling' as we are to eat meat, holiday in Israel or read a comic book. Our opinions are evidence-based; our actions driven by objectivity and cool analysis. This is the foundation stone of that rock solid belief system shared by people like us. It is the unstoppable accumulation of data, unimpeachable research, that turned us vegan, informed our support for the oppressed peoples of Palestine and strengthened our view that cartoons make you stupid. And yet, one day I had what I can only describe as an inkling . . .

The first little tingle, warning me that something disturbing was happening to me and you, came after that night out with Lee. You were walking ahead of me up the narrow pavement that led to our house and I knew you were angry about something and I presumed it was something to do with me. I knew you were angry because you neither complained about the hill ('This bloody thing. Why isn't there an electric trolley car or funicular or something to get us up here?') nor mentioned the stars ('You never see that many in the city, do you?'). Instead you trudged on in silence, leading the way, and I followed with a growing sense that there were words to be had as soon as we were indoors.

'Why did you say that about Lee's father?' you said as soon as I had locked the front door behind me.

I knew better than to reply immediately. Various actions—taking off my coat, hanging it on one of the hall hooks and moving to the kitchen—all gave me moments to think. There's a fine line between taking your time and refusing to answer but it is a skill you have allowed me to hone over the years. My equivalent of counting to ten has become: three actions, five paces. And speak.

'I'm sorry. What did I say?' I said, readying tap and kettle for my next pause.

'You know how sensitive they are about people talking behind their back. And paranoid,' you said.

I turned the tap on and filled the kettle, walked to place it on its base. Five steps. And said, honestly, 'Honestly, I have no idea what you are talking about.'

A risky tactic this but I felt secure, secure enough to face you with the smallest of smiles.

'You don't?' you said.

'Honestly, no,' I said, my honesty shining from my slightly smiling face and my open gestures. (Now that the kettle was on to boil, my hands were free to provide mimic back-up to my obvious innocence.)

'Lee, you said,' you said, 'How are things with your Dad? I hear you had quite a falling out, you said.'

O this was going to be easy, I thought. Tea bag in mugs, milk from fridge, dribble. Pace, pace, speak.

'Yes that is what I said,' I said.

'Why? Why would you say that?' you said.

'Because that is what you told me,' I said.

'What?' you said.

There was something about the look on your face at this point that gave me pause.

2. We go about our business, don't we? We guard the hive. We hover over the wide open upturned mouths of our many offspring and make sure the bugs in our beak are dropped into theirs in more or less equal portion. Patiently we gnaw at a log. Dutifully we leap upstream, migrate with the seasons, offer a paw when asked, use the flap provided to exit and enter the house. We all do our bit.

A student has said, 'Gatsby is a stalker. But he may have PTSD so we should forgive him.'

I thought about sharing this with you. You love Fitzgerald, after all. But what tone? What stance? Is this an astute observation? Does it reveal an interesting generational perspective that should amuse us, or intrigue us, show that either we were more sophisticated back then or were we so naïve that we were incapable of relating what we read in books to what we saw in the world around us? Should I shake my head and turn this into one of those kids-these-days moments that will bring us together, giggling like 20th Century schoolkids? Stalker! Would you believe? PTSD! I mean, I ask you!

I decided to say nothing. You were hunched over your laptop, pecking away at the keyboard with two fingers as if you were trying to disturb the worms that lived under there. Your long hair fell down and hid your eyes, your insulating concentration, that off-putting focus that I knew so well. It seemed a good idea to wait.

Finished with my tiny duties, I took a moment to wonder what it was that absorbed you so, what ogreish task held you tight in its grip. Perhaps you were beavering away . . . patiently we gnaw . . . beavering away at your witty snarky advice column. Sitting there pecking out imagined tales of reverse erectile malfunction or far-fetched cases of gender dysmorphia before passing around that wee poke of acid drops that you always have at hand. Did you think of the cruel advice first, I wondered, and then construct the ludicrous dilemma? Or was it more satisfying to first dream up all the awful disfiguring nightmare-inducing suffering that might befall people who were not us? Then ridicule them for it . . .

I considered the construction of a parody problem, a flimsy bridge over our current impasse. Dear You, Somebody close to you wishes to share something with you that you may find amusing. But they remember what happened last time. Eagerly, Me.

How long passed before I broke down and decided to speak? How long is a strand of hair?

'A student has said that Gatsby is stalker with PTSD,' I said.

The hair continued to hang, the fingers to peck.

'What do you think?' I said.

'About what?' you said into the keyboard.

'Gatsby,' I said.

'Gatsby,' you said. Hair. Peck.

'Yes,' I said.

'I don't know,' you said. 'I've never read it.'

3. I considered you a treat. I consider you a treat. I was aware that we had come to some sort of bump in the road, that some part of our life together had been tilted, but I refused to let whatever it was get in the way of that most basic of facts. You were, and will always remain, a gift. You are my prize for coming first in some race that I cannot remember entering. You are my award for reaching a pinnacle that I have no memory of climbing. There is something about what you mean to me that cannot be affected by our not always being on the same page.

When I was out at work, you remained in our home. More and more I found that I was thinking of you on those days, trying to imagine what part of the house you may be in, what attitude you were striking, what you were doing, what you may be thinking. Most often, I imagined you were at your desk in the small bedroom that we used as an office. I, too, was at my desk. As I was thinking of you, it seemed likely that you were thinking of me. My palm supported my cheek, elbow planted on the worn wooden surface, and this is how I saw you at home. Even from this distance, we mirrored each other. I felt certain.

There was no way I could check on this, of course. At least not with any degree of accuracy. If I came home and—following a suitable interval filled with those early evening activities that involved polite enquiry (cooking, eating, washing up, the news on TV)—I tried to, casually, drop into the conversation something along the lines of: can you remember exactly what you were doing at 2.20 this afternoon, then it was all too easy for me to guess how that particular conversation would pan out. Bewilderment, exasperation, even suspicion would be thrown in my direction and rightly so. It was in the best interests of both me and you that I simply assumed my feelings were accurate. At 2.20 you sat with your cheek in your palm and your elbow on the desk and you thought about me until you cramped up slightly. Absolutely extraordinary. Talk about two people being in synch!

4. Me and you stayed in a place somewhere in Rajasthan with a massive foetid heap just outside our bedroom window. Vultures worked their way around that steaming pile of crap all day long. Only me and you know what that smell was like. It can't be described; it can't be visited. Now it existed solely inside the two of us.

That was one of my thoughts that night that you were working late organising some award ceremony or other and I decided to cook something special, something nostalgic. Our senses have absorbed the same stuff. The art we have seen and heard . . . Bette Davis was screeching away at high volume as I chopped the ginger and chillies and I recalled me and you being delighted with her jerky leggy form, sitting in the dark at the BFI . . . the art we have seen and heard together worked in sedimentary fashion. Slowly, grain by grain, a relationship was formed.

And don't forget the tastes! It was as if I could hear you laughing in my ear as I rolled the smoked tofu in its miso dressing. How could I? How could we ever forget, me and you, the discoveries of food shared on our travels? This night was planned as a tribute to those many many times we had sat in an unlikely café, the only customers, as an ancient wrinkled proprietor cooked up a feast over a single flame. Places that can't be described; places that nobody we know will ever visit.

Touch has a memory, Keats said. There aint half been some clever bastards, Dury said. I was in an excellent mood.

I set the table, making sure to place a fork and spoon next to your chopsticks. You're a sport to try but it's something you've never picked up. I changed the music to Erik Satie and I remember I was just dimming the light switch in our front room when I heard your key in the door.

You went upstairs to change and I called out, 'Food on the table in five minutes.' There was an unusual sense of anticipation for me that night. I am not sure what it was. I had made an extra effort, true, but it wasn't that unusual. Only there was something about my musings as I cooked that made it feel like a special night for me.

I served the food in four large dishes placed in the centre of the dining table. Those pretty bowls we bought from Tangs department store in Singapore were empty and ready to be filled. 'Help yourself,' I remember I said. I noticed you looked a little strained and that you hadn't spoken since you came in but I was confident the feast I had prepared, specially mind, would soon cheer you up. I'm sure I'd be a bit grumpy if I ever had to plan something as preposterous as an award ceremony.

I watched you fill your own pretty bowl with noodles and vegetables and place some of the tofu on the top. Then you took your chopsticks and picked up a slithery piece of pak choy with an expertise that you have never possessed.

5. In my game you have to understand that interpretation is everything. Ownership and meaning are always up for grabs. It's a concept that I enjoy introducing to young minds, watch them struggle with it and then see that release of blessed relief when they get to grips with its implications. Nobody can ever tell us we are wrong! Authors don't own their texts, not once they hand it over to us. What matters are our feelings, our responses, what it means when it passes through the filter of us. You have to be able to back it up, I say. Yeah, whatever, they say. Bless them.

There is no fact not worth questioning. There is no such thing as an incontrovertible truth. Certainty is for villains; heroes have doubts. When two people tell me that Everest is the world's highest mountain, I assume that they are both telling me something different. There are, I am sure, as many concepts of height as there are people on the planet. The idea that something is more or greater than something else is such a challenging proposition that I am surprised that any agreement can ever be reached to decide the most basic competition. Don't get me started on sports. Or award ceremonies. For me *The Guinness*

Book Of Records is the most provocative book ever published. So my starting point on what we share as humans makes it difficult for me to accept that anything is ever truly shared.

But it's lonely, this outlook. No matter how appealing it may be to blow young minds with, something in my own philosophy denies my nature. It's intellectually cold and I am, I assure you, one of the warm ones.

So, romantically, I make room for the notion of two people who are so in tune with each other that they make joint memories. They travel to Nepal and they see the same mountain, give it the same name, link it to the same associations from their past. They hold hands and look up into the clouds and transfer emotions and impressions one to the other so that they can be shared with full mutual understanding until death. Outsiders may not agree with them or even believe them but the two will know. The two will always know.

6. 'Ow!' you said

'Something wrong?' I said

'What are you doing?' you said

'What do you mean?' I said

'That,' you said

'That?' I said

'Ow! Yes,' you said

'That's just the usual,' I said

'The usual?' you said

'Yes,' I said. 'This didn't seem an appropriate occasion for experimentation.'

'There is nothing usual about it,' you said

'You've gone off it?' I said

'Who could ever like something like that?' you said

'You've never complained before,' I said

'You've never done it to me before,' you said. 'Believe me, I would have complained. Loudly'

'Maybe you've changed a little', I said

'What do you mean?' you said

'Some sort of shift. An adjustment of sorts,' I said

'An adjustment?' you said

'Yes, perhaps. A change. A shift. A—let's call it—a realignment. You know. Inside,' I said

7. Places, please, everyone! Endings are choreography, well-drilled routines wherein each plucky member of the troupe plays a vital role. You need a strong opening, of course, but in Acts Two, Three and Four it goes unnoticed if you fluff a line or two, fumble a prop or miss an entrance here and there. But everything has to come together in an agreed pleasing fashion before we can all stand up in the light. We forgive those early mistakes in anticipation of the satisfaction to come.

We knew that a final act required willing, cooperative participants. There can be no slacking, no surprises, no rebellion. If Desdemona puts up a fight then we miss last orders. A delay to the train at that platform in Moscow leaves Anna kicking her heels. The impetus is lost. Our minds wander.

There is a corny geometry to endings. Witness the presence of Lee as our curtain came down. Lee—who may or may not have fallen out with their father—was essential; all acts of disintegration need to be observed by a third party. Shame needs a witness. Failure only occurs when somebody else is disappointed in you. Etcetera.

So Lee sat between us and they were forced to listen to versions of us. There was nothing out of the ordinary that I recall, just the usual small discrepancies: who said what, who did what, who refused to do what, who was amazed to realise that not doing something you don't want to do was now seen as some sort of transgression against our mighty ruler. It was all going along more or less as normal until that inevitable momentum that comes with socialising took over. Pleasantries must turn into conversation which must become a discussion and discussion requires illustration and that leads to story. And story in a social setting will, inevitably, birth anecdote and someone will give in to the seductive pull of performance.

On that occasion it was Lee—it had to be—who broke ranks and decided our amusement was their responsibility. They flapped and gurned their way through some predictable date-gone-awry saga. Either they or their prospective hook-up was awkward or rude or too short. I wasn't listening as I had already decided the best possible response, the perfect thing to say, as soon as an appropriate gap in their monologue appeared. I watched Lee stop to draw breath and then carry on a few times until eventually their closed lips seemed to signal some sort of ending. I swooped in. I turned to you.

'Sounds like a case for your advice column,' I said.

You looked at me. You could have painted a full scale Rivera mural on your expression.

'I haven't the faintest idea what you are talking about,' you said.

Were you waiting for me to speak again?

My silence was deep enough to bury a body.

currently

I wish to say something but I am concerned you may not be able to consider it

Why won't I?

I fear you may be distracted. You may not be able to offer your full attention

No. Not at all

Your mind is not elsewhere?

No. I am here. I promise. What did you wish to say?

Just that I admire people who never give up but I have no time for people who won't take no for an answer

Don't fret. You are neither of those

One of them is good, though

Sorry?

The first one. I said I admire them

It's hard to listen sometimes, isn't it?

Yes. Make up for it by saying something pleasant about me

You're very polite

Thank you

A considerate type

Yes. On that narrow pavement down to the town I always step into the road to let people pass. Have you noticed that?

I have noticed that

Whether I am facing towards the oncoming traffic or not

Putting yourself at risk for others

Whether or not they push a pram or use a . . . I have forgotten the name

Crutch

Stick. Whether or not they use a stick. Any age. I step out into the traffic

Often for no thanks

Often for no thanks

Very polite

Thank you. What are you reading?

A novel

Has it won awards?

Of course

Would you mind setting that book aside for a short time so that we may talk?

No not at all

That is wonderful. My previous friend would never do such a thing. My previous friend would make an unpleasant sound with their tongue to make me feel as if I had done something inconsiderate

Even though we have established that you are most considerate

Exactly

My previous friend showed similar inconsistencies

That's horrible. Even though we have established that you are amenable to other's needs. Even though you may wish to keep reading, you recognise that I wish you, for a short time probably but who knows . . .

That's true. I had no idea how long you wished to talk for when I set my award-winning novel aside

I may have been asking you to abandon it for the remainder of the night. But you didn't hesitate. You recognised my need and set your own aside like . . .

Like an award-winning novel I was enjoying

Exactly

. . .

We are doing fine, aren't we?

Yes. I am certain we are

We will know when we are not

I am certain of that

We have proved it, after all. Before

Yes. Both of us have proved it

I wanted to talk to you about what I said earlier

Go on

Do you remember when I said that I admired people who never gave up but I had no time for people who refused to take no for an answer?

Yes. I was reading. We were sitting as we are now

That's right

It was very recent

Yes

. . .

Well I am not sure I understand why . . . perhaps you will be able to make me understand over the course of this conversation . . . but I was hurt by your response

I am so sorry

Your lack of response rather

I can only apologise

Thank you. It hurt

May I ask what response you would have preferred? How may I not have hurt you?

Certainly. Let me . . .

Go on

I think I wished for some acknowledgement that I had said something clever

Clever

Yes. Some hint from you that you understood that there was considerable overlap between the groups of people involved. That admiring one group and dismissing the other could cause me some difficulty

I see. Yes that is clever. I am so sorry that I didn't notice it. I think I was reading at the time and, so, my attention was divided

I understand that

Thank you. Though I have to say that your reaction does come as something of a surprise

How so?

Well you are not a vain person

That is true. That is, I think it is fair to say, well-established

I thought so

I do not seek praise

Not at all

Remember, for instance, the time I won that award and I gave a short speech saying that I didn't deserve it. Most of those present were certain that my speech was sincere, a true reflection of my feelings

I wasn't there, I'm afraid

It was my previous friend

It must have been

You, however, have won an award when I was present, haven't you?

Yes. I won an award quite recently

And you gave a speech

Yes. I gave a short speech saying I didn't deserve it

I believed it was sincere

Thank you. I believe I really meant it

And another thing worth noticing

What's that?

I wasn't jealous then. Nor am I now

That's wonderful to hear

Good. This lack of jealousy, along with my politeness, rank amongst my admirable qualities

Yes they do

Odd, then, that my lack of vanity didn't save me from that recent hurt

Yes it is

Do you have any explanation? I am really at sea here

Well it does remind me a little of my previous friend

How so?

They professed to have a sense of humour and would occasionally be hurt if I did not appreciate a joke

How tiresome

Yes it was

Oddly, your reaction also reminded me of my previous friend

That seems a remarkable coincidence

Doesn't it?

How can I possible be like them?

O I assure you you are not! Heavens!

But in this one instance?

Yes. On this occasion I was reminded of them. How they would not listen to something I said that could be considered witty

And when you have to repeat it then that lessens the effect of your witticism

Naturally. It is diluted beyond repair like . . .

A spoiled summer drink. One of those in a jug filled to the brim with ice that is left out on a table in the garden for too long before the guests finish it. The first couple of glasses are delicious but then . . .

Spoiled. Watery

Just slush

A terrible shame

. . .

. . .

Does it affect you in any way when I say you remind me, in some aspects, on rare occasions, of my previous friend?

Yes, I must say that I do feel something

What do you feel, may I ask?

It is difficult to describe

Can you try?

. . .

For me?

Well. It is not exactly hurt. It does not feel the same as when you, in effect, ignore me . . .

I am so sorry

. . . by not taking the time to understand something I may have taken some time to prepare

I am so sorry

It is more akin to a small irritation like . . .

A small patch of reddened skin near the top of the shoulder. One that is easy to reach but you wish were a little easier

Yes. Exactly like that

I am so sorry

It irks me when you say that I remind you of your previous friend. I am nothing like them. I have never met them

Actually you have

I have?

Yes. You two did meet

Under what possible circumstances could I have met your previous friend?

It was when I won my first award, do you remember?

This was not a recent event?

No it was some time ago

Did you give a short speech saying how you didn't deserve it?

Yes I did

Yes I do remember. I remember I believed you meant it

Thank you. I believe I was being sincere

Sincerity . . . and I am not sure I have said this to you . . . is one of your admirable qualities

Thank you

And your previous friend was present at this event?

They were

Extraordinary

And you spoke with them briefly

Good Lord!

You told them that you felt that I deserved my award

I did? Well you did

Thank you

And did they agree?

They made no comment

How rude!

Yes. My previous friend became rude

Often?

Often. It became one of their bad traits

Mine too

Rudeness?

Often. My previous friend could be very cutting

In public?

Yes. In front of other people

Often?

Yes

I am pleased I never witnessed that

No. You are lucky. You never met my previous friend

Not even when you were accepting an award?

No. There was no such occasion

Why is that?

You have won many more awards than me

O. Of course

. . .

How odd that we have never met in the street, though

That is odd

This is such a small place, after all

Yes. Odd that you have never, for example, had to move out of their way so that they may carry on up or down the narrow pavement

You feel that I would step into the traffic?

I am certain of it

No matter which direction I was facing?

I am certain. My previous friend would show no such consideration

They sound so difficult

They were

Mine too

Difficult?

Very

You know . . .

What is it?

This may seem an unsuitable thought

Tell me

Very well. You know I find it comforting when we discuss those traits in our previous friends that we find . . .

Unpleasant

. . . challenging

Yes I also find that comforting

It feels like . . .

. . . soaking in a warm bath at the end of one of those days, one of those days when you may have, say, received an award and you have had to be on your best behaviour for hours, meeting people you may not know well or at all, dressed so that you do not cause comment, having to make sure that everybody understands that you think you didn't deserve it, the chatter, the fixed smile that makes your teeth and cheekbones ache, the speech that says you don't deserve it, the comments that you sounded sincere and the thanks that follow, the gossip about other ones that makes you wish to scream, the longing in your body for solitude, and then you come home and close a door, you open another door, you fill the tub, you close another door and you are alone and it is over and it has gone as planned so the relief in your body and mind and the warm water come together like . . .

. . .

Like that

. . .

. . .

You know that a trait you possess that is rarely acknowledged as one of your admirable qualities is your willingness to recognise, speedily, when you have made a mistake, phrased something a little carelessly or acted without sufficient thought

Is it?

Yes it is. Yet this trait is never mentioned when people come together and discuss you and your character

Do people come together to do that? It is difficult to imagine

It is not difficult to imagine at all. Think! At an award ceremony in your honour, for example, it is only natural that the people gathered there would discuss you when you are out of earshot

Where might I be?

Elsewhere. In the bathroom perhaps perfecting your acceptance remarks so that we will be absolutely convinced that you believe you do not deserve your award

And, while I am doing that, people discuss my qualities?

Good and bad

. . .

Mostly good

. . .

Yet I am certain they never mention your efficient facility for apology

. . .

Which, to me, seems a great shame

Yes

Perhaps next time people gather to celebrate you and your works and you have disappeared for a time to prepare your remarks then I will raise this matter and ensure that it is recognised as a quality of yours that is to be placed on the plus side of your register

Thank you. I would appreciate that

We are doing fine, aren't we?

Yes we will know when we are not, I am certain

We have always known before, haven't we?

Always

. . .

. . .

I may resume my reading now

Very well

This has been very useful. Fulfilling

I think so

Well worth taking the time away from my award-winning book

But. . .

Yes?

Before you return to your reading I wish to say something

Certainly

Whilst I have your full attention

Of course

I wanted to say that I admire openness in people but I have no time for those who share their thoughts, opinions and feelings with others

That is a position which presents you with some difficulty

Yes

Because people who are open are nearly always those who share their thoughts, opinions and feelings with others

Exactly

Very clever

Thank you

Well done

There's no need for praise, honestly

You deserve it

No. No really

Shortly

Again!

The little brown dog

WHY?

Because they like small dogs and had one that colour when they were little

WHY?

Because their Mummy and Daddy wanted them to have a pet

WHY?

To teach them how to look after a living thing

AGAIN!

The little brown dog

WHY?

Because it hasn't got a name yet

WHY?

Because the family cannot agree on a name

WHY?

Because they often disagree and find it hard to come to a decision on anything

AGAIN!

No, it's my turn

Very well

AGAIN!

The little brown dog

WHY?

Because

AGAIN!

The little brown dog

WHY?

Because

AGAIN!

AN INTERVIEW WITH JESSE SALVO

Blue Rhinoceros, a story that follows a town's quick and harrowing descent into madness in the wake of an industrial disaster, is Jesse Salvo's debut novel. Though he normally writes short stories and captures the attention of literary magazine aficionados, Salvo takes a break from his normal prose to create a work of art that forces us to reckon with our shortcomings both as a society and at the atomized individual level. The audience, when reading, is invited to compare their own moral and philosophical standing to the sad, hapless cast of characters that populate the story. I had the opportunity to sit down with Salvo and discuss his novel in detail. Below are the ramblings of a genius, or perhaps a madman. I suppose only time will tell.

In your own words, how would you summarize your book?

"A whodunnit for the death of a species." is what I sheepishly tell people at parties when they ask. In my experience, they are almost never impressed with that explanation.

What would you say was your biggest inspiration for starting the novel?

Great question! Depends what you mean. Stylistically, I always reach back for Joseph Mitchell's nonfiction work. The prose is basically just me doing a Joseph Mitchell impression. Gabriel Garcia Marquez and Raymond Chandler are influences (though strange bedfellows, I guess). Also a wonderful play called *Rhinoceros* by Eugene Ionesco.

Philosophically, different story. The book has a philosophical scaffolding that I don't necessarily agree with, but my weakness as a writer is now, and ever shall be, structure, and I find once I commit in advance to a totalizing worldview, even one that I'm not 100% on board with, it clarifies a lot for me, and gives me some breathing room to explore character. From there, I can play around testing the fences of that philosophy. The ur-text that undergirds the whole book is a series of University lectures called *The Variety of Religious Experience* by William James. James chronicled the reported experiences of mystics, fanatics, people who'd experienced stigmata, etc. A great deal of the character Sairy is a sort of amalgamated, more sinister, version of James' secondhand saints. The book also engages a lot with anarchist philosophy, especially through the character Robert Vicaray. I don't come from a philosophy background so my understanding of some of this stuff was a bit callow, but to give the *appearance* of depth, I read some Murray Bookchin, David Graeber (who I'd already admired quite a bit) and a bit of Bakunin obviously.

How did Covid-19 affect your writing process? Your end product?

Well the whole of this novel was written over the course of about 3 months in Sevilla during the national confinement here. You couldn't leave your house except to go to the hospital or get groceries. Every night people would bang pots and pans to support hospital workers. Other than that, it was silent. The Mercado de Feria, which had been operating every Thursday since the 13th century, ceased operating. After the confinement ended we couldn't leave the country because the backup in the Immigration offices was such that they weren't going to be able to process visas for maybe 6 months. So I had a bunch of unstructured time, I was kind of trapped like a lot of other expats. Australians, other Americans, etc. We were all living on savings in a nine person house in a pueblo near Valencia. Rent was 200 euros. We made communal dinners, and I ate a lot of canned vegetables. Writing at that moment felt like an act of such radical optimism. The idea that there would be another year, and a year after that, and that in those years someone might pick up a book and begin reading it for leisure. So I wrote a lot. It was all I could think to do. Now I'm a bit burned out from it, but hopefully the feeling will come back.

How did living in Spain influence the journey of this novel? From writing, to publishing, to promotion?

It had a big impact on the language of the book. Speaking Spanish every day changes your relationship to English whether you want it to or not. For me, it's been a huge asset. It's allowed me to experiment more on the sentence level.

Living here can also lend a bit of critical distance which is helpful sometimes in assessing the United States and U.S. political horizons. The obvious example is Europeans find for-profit healthcare barbaric.

I didn't attend an MFA program, so I don't have a real community of U.S. authors I belong to. I've heard a few writers over the years say something to the effect of: they want to find their Paris. As in Ernest Hemingway and Ezra Pound, or maybe as in Van Gogh and Lautrec. No offense meant, but that's not really attractive to me. I have decidedly limited interest in surrounding myself with a bunch of other writers who are trading *bon mots* or whatever. Reading and writing are both solitary exercises. You have to be alone in a room with yourself. I'd much rather find my Arles. Stay out in the wilderness.

Did you always think or know the main animal for the book would be a rhinoceros? Were there any other possible options?

I think it was always a rhino. I had already tried the idea out as a short story, but in the short story format the killing of the rhinoceros felt like it overpowered everything else. I figured it was a failure, so I shelved it. When COVID hit, it sort of snuck back up on me. I think the idea originally sprung from reading the reporting about some of the last African white rhinos. In particular I think the podcast Radiolab had done a story about some rich asshole who'd bid at a conservation

auction to basically go to Africa to hunt and kill an old white rhino. I remember how they described the guy finally killing it, and how almost banal the killing was. The rhino was just standing there, and the rich guy had bad aim, so he only wounded it first. There was no dramatic charge or clash between man and beast or whatever Kipling-adjacent fantasy the rich fellow had in his head. It boiled down to this sort of very slow, clumsy execution of one of the last members of a species.

Are there any events in the book that you took inspiration from your own life and adapted into the writing? If so, what?

Maybe some of Oscar Louder's dourness, especially concerning elite universities. I've done some direct-relief work, though nothing like what's described in the book. The 92 Expo, which in the book takes place in New York, actually did take place in Seville, and like in the book they created these massive white elephant structures just outside the city (including a spaceship) and then abandoned them all. It's a very strange place to walk through.

At what point did you know you were done with the book? Was it part of a process? Or was there a final day of writing?

I finished it one day in the kitchen of that shared house in that pueblo. I don't know how I knew it was done except there seemed to be nothing more I had to say. It was dreadful. Can't wait to do it again.

What do you want readers to take away from your novel?

I guess if the novel had an actual project, it was to create a grammar for understanding and expressing just how grim manmade climate change is, and will be going forward. You can say 150 species a day, or 3 degrees centigrade, but fundamentally our brains don't or can't register that reality. So if the empirical reality has proved too overwhelming, or too abstract, I wanted to create a new emotional grammar. That is what the novel aims to do, especially in those last chapters, to create a new mode of expression since the old modes seem to come up short.

Do you see this project branching off into any other works? Will this remain a singular novel?

I can't imagine returning to this world again. Maybe a character or two will pop up somewhere else, who knows. Dave Boggs I quite like, despite everything.

What plans do you have for your next big publishing project?

When I know I'll tell you. I'm really superstitious about discussing anything prior to it being finished. I have one other novel MS kicking around. It predates *Blue Rhinoceros* by three or four years, so it might be fun to go back and see if there's anything there.

What are you most proud of regarding the process of writing the novel and having it published?

I think the responses it's gotten from readers who don't know me at all. That's really gratifying because you never know how the voice is going to hit someone who has no context for you. Friends and family are always going to read you more charitably, give you the benefit of the doubt. It's been a thrill to receive positive feedback from readers who came to it cold.

What was the most difficult part about becoming published?

God, the editing is a nightmare! I'm not very doctrinaire about grammar, and editors, it turns out, are. But promotion is hands down my least favorite thing. Every time I send out another chain email I feel like I'm selling NFTs.

Do you have anyone you would love to give a shout out (that you already have within the book or that you couldn't make room for on the back page)?

I feel terrible having forgotten him in the Acknowledgements, but my friend Pat Spagnuolo. Pat, I love you! My friend Adrian, in Spain, my only writer friend here. Also, Ben Drevlow at Bull who gave me my first fiction editor position. He is perhaps the most charitable person in the literary world, I honestly don't know how Ben does it.

What character do you relate to the most in the book?

Yikes. I mean the correct answer is that they're all me, right? Maybe Beebop. I would say I have a lengthy intro where I implore readers not to confuse me for the narrator. Everyone in my life who read the book ignored that directive.

What part of the book was the most difficult for you to research and find information on?

The logistics of the maple flood. I took a long, long time trying to crunch numbers on what that would look like. That said, I recently got an email from a retired physicist who'd finished the book and said that he'd been skeptical. Then, after some back-of-the-envelope math, he determined that I'd mostly nailed it. That was nice to hear. That said the book's not exactly striving for accuracy.

When did you first want to become a writer and why?

I can't say when exactly. Maybe age 12, the first time I picked up *The Hobbit*. I also recall reading some quote from the novelist Tom Robbins about how half his family had been revival tent preachers, and the other half traveling soap salesmen, so you couldn't say he didn''t come by his trade honestly. Something like that. The truth is, I'm not good for much else, in a practical sense. I despise honest work. This was the only club that would take me.

Birth of Eros
Debra Di Blasi
KERNPUNKT, Nov 2022

The 1950s hold a contested place in the American psyche like few other eras. Scorned in contemporary classics such as Sloan Wilson's *The Man in the Gray Flannel Suit* and Richard Yates' *Revolutionary Road* for its supposed emphasis on conformity, the decade has since undergone a rehabilitation of sorts as an era of hidden progress and ferment. Historian David Halberstam's *The Fifties* is a decade that gave birth to the pill, not just *Ozzie and Harriet*; *The Story of a Marriage* in Andrew Sean Greer's 1950s-set novel of that name is also the saga of a decade of percolating secrets far more complex that those exposed in *Peyton Place*. And now, just as most Americans who remember the 1950s spend much of their leisure time trying to recall where they have placed their reading glasses, experimental novelist Debra Di Blasi serves up a take on the period so fresh and outré that, upon reading it, Dwight Eisenhower might suffer yet another heart attack from beyond the grave.

Di Blasi's *Birth of Eros* begins with the birth of Lucy, a homely infant ("nose lips cheeks jaw brow bone somehow wrong") who enters Los Angeles in 1952 with a "left eye squinty from past ancestors" and a right eye "bulged with future progeny." The right eye—"My Right Eye," capitalized to its own identity—affords Lucy a panoramic view of the present and a periscopic bead on the future, allowing for the proleptical asides that distinguish the novella's structure. Soon the reader learns, as does Lucy, that she has been thrust straight from the birth canal into the belly of the rollicking plot.

Lucy's mother, Beauty, a stunning brunette ("Mannequin with breath, with wet. Lickable lips of mouth and cunt. A dream, a girl machine, a living doll") has found employment with a shady automotive dealer, Big Bad Wolf, who seeks to transform her into the Dinah Shore of Fords, albeit one who far more resembles a teenage Veronica Lake. He also pressures Beauty into posing for X-rated photos which he sells to his "rich suckass pals." Wolf's undoing begins when he recruits Lucy's future father ("tan pecs and overstuffed genitals"), a former underwear model once billed as "Tarzan of the Cosmopolitan Jungle," to play Beauty's husband in the showroom. The father had been blacklisted from newspaper ads over his mammoth organ, and as a result, he "no longer wore underwear, out of spite." He reassured himself: "I'll make the whole undie industry go bust by showin' 'em panties are for girls."

Alas, Beauty fails to recognize that her stage husband is not intended for her genuine mate. She is, after all, despite her beauty, a lonely girl who'd "stuff a man's leather glove with cotton and slip it into her jacket pocket and hold it tight and go for a walk talking and holding hands with the glove of a man not there who she'd love better than best if he'd only just be . . ." Hence Lucy. Hence an innocent witness to this ill-fated pas de trois. In Lucy's own words, "Lower math: Three plus one equals misery. Especially if one is a motherfucking car dealing money laundering pornmonger."

Or maybe not so innocent. Like Oskar in *The Tin Drum*, Lucy is both child and adult, alive with a constant state of naïve wonder and yet wise to the ways of the world. She is named after Lucille Ball, the star of her father's beloved sitcom, *I Love Lucy*. Yet she is also aware of her other nominal forebear, Saint Lucia of Syracuse, the Christian virgin who was defiled and had her "eyes torn out" and her neck hitched to oxen yoke." In *Birth of Eros*,

Lucy proves herself an eager, animated narrator at once fascinated and detached from her family's undoing.

Di Blasi has a gift for grappling with challenging, timeless questions of ethics and justice, yet doing so in a manner that is neither hackneyed nor didactic. Lucy demands: "Define beauty. Give me the facts, the science, the phenomenon: Geometric perfection to electrify mathematicians . . . ? Tell me the function of beauty beyond titillation, beyond the buy & sell . . . " She probes: "Who deserves to die? Where do you draw the line between abiding life and causing death? Which crime's that Nth worse, that breath too much wind against the tightrope walker?" In lesser hands, these lines of inquiry might run the risk of transforming Birth of Eros into a novella of ideas. Yet the orchestrated chaos that surrounds these investigations—and that ultimately sees one character hogtied inside the trunk of a sedan—renders these moments into welcome palate cleansers of an intellectual bent. The result is a novella of ideas tucked into a comedy of manners and folded between the sheets of a satiric heist saga.

Di Blasi's gift for lyrical prose ranks her among our most nimble wordsmiths, an author whose voice sings in a thousand different tunes—and yet remains distinctly recognizable. The verbal antics in her description of "fathermother's" employer's sexual shortcomings give a sense of how her prose sizzles:

> Big Bad Wolf knew the depraved cravings of men. Knew his own sewn from the want of big cock more than of little cunt. Knew he'd never have the big

to get the little, thus never get the whole balla wax. Never be the cat's pajamas, cat's meow—not even the cat, for that matter, fat cat though he was, with dough rising high in the Los Angeles sky like exhaust fumes from tailpipes of the thousand-plus automobiles he sold each year at the Sale-O-Rama.

With the caveat that some readers may find the juxtaposition of this electrifying language and the underlying content, especially episodes of sexual exploitation, disquieting, the contrast does serve its purposes, and the effect is as powerful as it proves unsettling. Lucy is the rare narrator who can capture the panoply of human sexuality without either shame or guilt, and the frank poetry of sex allows readers to form their own judgments. Di Blasi's southern California striptease is not Holden Caulfield's 1950s anymore—and thank the gods of Eros for that.

Innovative high jinks are hard to pull off in any literary form, but especially within the narrow confines of the novella. There's a reason *Tristram Shandy* weighs in over six hundred pages and the average Pynchon novel can sink a small battleship. Setting such a daring novella against the backdrop of an already well-mined era, and peppering the prose with erotic imagery as seen from the point of view of an omniscient infant until the plot catches flame with the intensity of nitrate film, seems rather an ambitious task. That Di Blasi's *Birth of Eros* rises to the occasion, and ensures the subsequent conflagration draws us in like primordial fire, is testament to the author's searing imagination and red-hot literary courage.

The Last Days
Ali Millar
Ebury Press (UK), July 2022

It was 2010 in leafy Blackford, Edinburgh, when a Jehovah's Witness and his two restless preschoolers appeared on my doorstep to serve me their particular mangling of the New Testament. I summarily rebuffed my unwanted visitors by stating plainly that I was an atheist unlikely to be swayed by their flimsy pamphlets, and anyway wasn't it written in Leviticus that [some clever petard-hoisting zinger]. Correction. I summarily rebuffed them by pretending I had lamb on the stove that required careful monitoring lest my shanks lose their succulence. A moment later, the fellow re-chapped the door to ask if his pained-looking young daughter could use my toilet. I stood aside as the pair occupied the bathroom for ten minutes, leaving an unholy stink in the room upon exit. My abiding memory of God's Chosen People, then, is the sorrowful eyes of a bored toddler upon leaving an excremental whiff in my small flat, thereby helping to create my strained yet apt analogy that the Witnesses politely invade your inner sanctum, stay there for far too long, and leave a lingering shitty stench that never seems to fade.

In Millar's lyrical memoir of leaving the cult, we follow her long and painful upbringing as her mercurial mother whelps her into their wacky nontrinitarian ways. Across a series of intimately written chapters, where the narrative voice seamlessly captures the troubled interior of her younger self as she moves from innocence to rebellion, Millar explores the suffocating blandness and the pernicious weirdness of their beliefs (refusing blood transfusions or meat that has not been bled in Jehovah's preferred manner). The most shocking section sees Millar, then married with child in her late twenties, interrogated by two "elders" about her marital transgressions, an excruciating and humiliating scene in which the sinister creeps clearly revel in the erotic detail.

In the *Guardian* review, Rachael Cooke wrote on how she strained to "fully sympathise with her [Millar's] inability to leave the sect", and that she "could not quite picture her mother, or her husband, or the elders". This misunderstands the writer's stylistic intent, methinks. The people with whom Millar should share a natural intimacy are kept at a constant distance, mirroring the distance at which these emotionally stunted people keep their children or partners, reserving their maximum love for Jehovah and serving up criticisms of ungodly actions as a substitute for that unoffered love. The recall of her sexual discovery with Original Simon, her first lover, and the chapters exploring her nascent teenage rebellion bring that missing rush of intensity and warmth that Cooke bemoans back into the prose. How the Witnesses continually break free from their tethers of propriety and temporarily live, only to find themselves snapped back into familiar self-suppressing behaviours, is repeatedly fascinating. Cooke also suggests "that her childhood hurts too much to be properly accounted for", i.e. Cooke's inability to emotionally connect with the book is entirely the fault of the author and her unreadiness to properly tell her story at the correct emotional bandwidth for maximum literary truthiness.

Millar's narrative non-fiction debut explores how the tentacles of a cult run deep, in an elegant, startling, and sublimely hewn style.

Here Goes Nothing
Steve Toltz
Melville House (US) /
Sceptre (UK), May 2022

Sydney's black sheep Steve Toltz, now resident in Los Angeles, publishes sparsely (three novels in fifteen years—the first, *A Fraction of the Whole*, is an extravagant anti-saga, the second,

Quicksand, a caffeinated classic evoking Stanley Elkin), but always serves up satisfying novels of unflinching misanthropy and cathartic black comedy. In *Quicksand*, the reader is taken on a blistering *voyage au bout de la nuit* to the darkest recesses of existence, at the core of which sits Toltz, snickering like an imp at the horrors and pratfalls of the human race, howling for kicks into the void. His hilarious pronouncements on life are beautiful koans, insane stand-up routines, hyperbolic rambles, tasteless shockers, and long monologues featuring razor-sharp and sublimely honed prose mastery.

In this one, ex-crim Angus and shock-pastor Gracie welcome the terminally ill Owen into their home as a permanent resident in exchange for the dying's man worldly possessions. Very swiftly into this macabre arrangement, Owen murders Angus, who vaporises into a bardic halfway house for the newly dead and proceeds to watch as the vile interloper wheedles his way into his marital bed. The novel alternates between the disappointing afterlife where one's financial obligations continue and Angus takes work as an umbrella salesman, while Gracie's oncoming pregnancy results in a hilarious and shocking scene of a self-performed caesarean section where instructions are fed to her from the chat in a livestream. There is an apocalyptic flavour to the novel as the new pandemic K9, transmitted by dogs with a kill rate over 80%, spreads swiftly across the world, leaving Gracie with the problem of keeping her newborn alive in an unliveable world. As always with Toltz, the dialogue is wildly dyspeptic, the pace frenetic, and the style serves up an unapologetically bleak and bitter honesty that verges on the transcendent, making Toltz one of the world's most powerful contemporary writers.

Winter Recipes from the Collective
Louise Glück
Farrar, Straus and Giroux, 2021

I must ask your forbearance in advance for nattering on about the Nobel Prize before diving into a review of Louise Glück's most recent book.

A winner of the Nobel Prize in Literature has nothing to prove. It's not only the highest monetary award a writer can receive, it's also the most universal, in theory being open to anyone in the world. Because there is usually only one award per year (in 1904, 1917, 1966 and 1974 there were two), there can be controversy and contention when the committee in Sweden announces its annual decision. Most often this is not because the recipient is viewed as unworthy, but rather because other candidates are seen by some as even more worthy. On the other hand, sometimes the award simply makes people scratch their heads. In an elegy for Philip Roth, who never got a Nobel, *New Yorker* Editor David Remnick wrote: "Recently, when I asked him what he thought of Bob Dylan's Nobel Prize, he said, 'It's O.K., but next year I hope Peter, Paul and Mary get it.'"

I want to throw out some Nobel Prize stats the way a baseball lover tosses around numbers about his favorite game. Between 1901 and 2021 there have been 118 Nobel Prizes in Literature awarded. There have been seven years when no prize was given (1914, 1918, 1935 and 1940–43). This was somewhat offset by the four years when the award was split between two writers. Only 15 women writers have received it, or 12.7% of the total. Four of those came in the first 60 years of the prize, 11 in the last 60 years, so the odds for women have been improving, but are still nowhere near even. Overall, you could make a pretty good drinking game out of all the writers who deserved to win and never did.

I mention these facts because they highlight just how remarkable Louise Glück's achievement is. At a time when arguably more than half of the best writers in the world are women, they remain behind the eight ball when it comes to the Nobel Prize. To win, you must live long enough to produce an impressive body of work and also to have it be fully recognized. You can't die brilliant and prolific but young like Federico Garcia Lorca, James Wright or Anne Sexton. At the same time, having made it to a ripe old age and produced a lot of great work, you must still be clinging to life when they nominate you.

All right, I've got that out of my system. Now I can say that anyone who questions whether Louise Glück deserved to win the Nobel in 2020 should read her latest book, *Winter Recipes from the Collective*. It may be the best thing she's ever done, which is saying quite a bit. The first thing to notice about it is how brief it is—15 poems in a mere 42 pages. In most quarters it would be called a chapbook, not a full-length collection. While Glück has always practiced the art of less-is-more, the concision of this volume speaks volumes. And yet a number of the poems are longer, employing multiple sections like many of those in her previous book, *Faithful and Virtuous Night* (2014). Whatever their length, more often than not their power comes from what is not said, from what can't be said in the face of disease, death and loss. The specific personal occasion for these verses is the sickness and death of her only surviving sister (another died before Louise was born), and the growing awareness of her own mortality that this event and old age bring to her.

Emotionally, this book feels closest to *Meadowlands* (1996), which dealt with the disintegration of a marriage through a loose retelling of *The Odyssey*. What has changed since then? Glück's fierce intelligence, ever-present and off-putting

to some (though not to lovers of hard truths), continues to guide her singing toward greater spareness, allowing thoughts, feelings and images to rise from her psyche seemingly without interference or judgment, except of course in their arrangement. The effect is that her free verse, always quietly melodious and graceful, feels simultaneously freer and more focused than ever before. There is a haiku-like richness and suggestiveness to so many of these plainspoken lines. From "Autumn":

> Life, my sister said,
> is like a torch passed now
> from the body to the mind.
> Sadly, she went on, the mind is not
> there to receive it.

From "The Denial of Death":

> Everything is change, he said, and everything is
>   connected.
> Also everything returns, but what returns is not
> what went away—

From "An Endless Story":

> The Chinese were right, she said, to revere the old.
> Look at us, she said. We are all of us in this room
> still waiting to be transformed. This is why we
>   search for love.
> We search for it all of our lives,
> even after we find it.

From "Night Thoughts":

> All too soon I emerged
> my true self,
> robust but sour,
> like an alarm clock.

I wish the copyright laws would allow me to quote even one of these poems in full, say, the shortest one, "A Sentence," a masterpiece of compression and heartbreak at only nine lines. As you can gather from the selections quoted, many of the poems take the form of conversations—between the author and her sister, the author and a lover, the author and death (also a lover?), the author and a teacher. "The Setting Sun" is cast as a dialogue with a teacher of painting. Did Glück ever study painting? Or is this a way of writing about her poetry mentors, Stanley Kunitz and Léonie Adams? Or is it a metaphor for the spiritual journey, or some combination of all of these? I don't know. I also think it doesn't matter, though it's fun and irresistible to speculate. Most likely this is another classic Louise Glück move, transforming her life into myth so as to better make the personal universal. Among several surprises in the poem, it turns out the painting teacher "has been blind for many years" (!). However, this apparently does not hinder him from teaching the visual arts:

> As to my current predicament: when I judge from
>   a student's
> despair and anger he has become an artist,
> then I speak. Tell me, he added,
> what do you think of your own work?
> Not enough night, I answered. In the night I can
>   see my own soul.
> That is also my vision, he said.

I have now read this book five times. I'm sure I'll reread it many more times if I live long enough. Each time it has brought tears to my eyes—tears for its austere yet human beauties, and tears for its sorrows. From beginning to end it is captivating, provocative and haunting. Three more brief quotes if I may. From the first poem, coincidentally called "Poem":

> And the world goes by,
> all the worlds, each more beautiful than the last;

From the title poem, which also illuminates the title:

> . . . The book contains
> only recipes for winter, when life is hard. In spring,
> anyone can make a fine meal.

And from the end of the last poem, "Song":

> Ah, he says, you are dreaming again

> And I say then I'm glad I dream
> the fire is still alive

Indeed it is! A Nobel Prize-winner has nothing to prove, but an artist always has something to prove, if only to herself. If you buy this book and read the entire poem, you'll see that it starts out with normal punctuation, periods and whatnot. By the end, though, there are no more periods, only commas, and in the final two lines not even those. The fire still burns yet in writing about death she has learned something about letting go, both creatively and spiritually. For me those last two lines are emblematic of the whole movement of this brief, brilliant book.

The Best-Laid Plans of Rhinos and Men

Blue Rhinoceros
Jesse Salvo
New Meridian Arts, 2022

The central premise of *Blue Rhinoceros*—Jesse Salvo's darkly humorous debut—revolves around a murder in a small town in upstate New York. One of the many peculiar pleasures of this multi-layered, elliptically constructed novel is that it comes wrapped—misleadingly—in the outward trappings of a classic gumshoe detective thriller. A well-dressed dame walks through the door, seeking to hire a world-weary investigator to look into a mysterious and largely forgotten crime. In Chandleresque fashion, as old witnesses are interviewed and mossy rocks overturned, the scope of the investigation expands into increasingly sinister territory, implicating the hidden machinations of the highest echelons of industry and government, and the devious entities who work behind the scenes to protect the interests of the powerful and the wealthy.

But *Blue Rhinoceros* isn't a gumshoe detective thriller, and to the credit of its author, it doesn't really pretend to be one either. Salvo is after something more original and substantial than the gimmick of subverting a well-trod genre. Although populated by a cast of delightfully eccentric characters subjected to an outlandish cascade of improbable crises, the novel grapples with serious moral and ethical concerns, casting a grim eye on the flawed nature of humanity and our uncertain collective fate.

So. The present year is 2030, but this isn't a science fiction novel either, and the world of the near future seems much like the world of the present, if slightly worse for wear. The rich dame in the doorway is Sairy Wellcomme, a professional zoologist, young but well-regarded in her field. The door she walks through belongs to the squalid, one-room cabin of Thomas Entrecarceles, who is not a private dick, but a former journalist—once a household name, but now, due to a well-publicized scandal in his career, so disgraced that he can't even find work bagging groceries. The crime Sairy is willing to pay Thomas to investigate took place seventeen years ago in her hometown of Littoral, NY: the murder of Beebop, the last living African blue rhinoceros on earth.

As it turns out, Sairy already knows who murdered Beebop. She did, at the age of 12, exactly two days after both her parents died in a terrible accident. What Sairy wants Thomas to investigate is *why* she murdered the last blue rhinoceros. She has no memory whatsoever of the event.

Thus is established the central mystery that spins the Rube Goldberg plot into motion. The course of the novel will swing back and forth between Thomas's present-day sleuthing in 2030—sifting through old news archives on the internet, tracking down witnesses all over the back roads of New York State—and his reconstruction of the preposterous chain of events that unfolded in 2012, culminating in the death of a rhinoceros at the hands of a 12-year-old girl.

Early in his investigation, Thomas discovers that Sairy's parents died on a particularly significant day in the history of Littoral. As it happens, many, many other townspeople were also killed that day, in a catastrophic industrial accident so memorably bizarre and grotesque that I'll refrain from spoiling it for readers.

The events of that day will be revisited, over and over, from a wide range of divergent perspectives. In the process we will be introduced to a motley assortment of offbeat characters—all, in some way, deformed by their traumatic pasts, and all, in some way, responsible for inflicting trauma upon others. We'll meet a despairing pet shop owner ruined by a hurricane. A preternaturally gifted child who breaks a blind prisoner out of jail with the aid of a canoe. A sociopathic corporate spy, fond of prosthetic noses and fake beards, who may or may not work for the CIA. And we will spend a great deal of time with the Rude Mechanicals, an off-the-grid cabal of outlaw activists devoted to providing humanitarian aid at various national disasters around the country, founded by a trio of odd bedfellows: Robert Vicaray, environmentalist and accidental millionaire; Oscar Louder, an embittered insurance adjuster; and Sam Herbert, a nebbishy financial whiz-kid. All of their paths will lead to the Pavilion of the Abandoned Future, and at the center of it all lies the mystery of Sairy Wellcomme and the last blue rhinoceros.

(By the way, I should note that outside of this eponymous novel—at least as far as I can determine from my very cursory internet research—there is no such creature as a blue rhinoceros, African or otherwise. But Salvo takes great care to make us believe there is such a creature, and he certainly had me convinced.)

This is a novel strewn with marvelously absurd catastrophes, but for the unfortunate characters of *Blue Rhinoceros*, the undeniable absurdity of the tragedies that befall them only adds insult to injury. This is, indeed, one of the recurrent themes of the novel—that unexpected disasters happen to ordinary people all the time, but we look away and tell ourselves such experiences are anomalous, exceptional, because they don't fit into the reassuring narratives we have built our lives around. American popular culture—largely shaped by self-serving capitalist interests—has conditioned us to believe that so long as we work hard and play by the rules, we will be duly rewarded with our fair share of prosperity, comfort, and safety. But when bad things happen, the façade is ripped away, exposing the American Dream for the empty illusion it is and always has been.

When you consider, in aggregate, the astonishing daily headlines generated in the real world, the freakish calamities of *Blue Rhinoceros* don't seem so far-fetched. In a Connecticut suburb, a reclusive, mentally-ill young man, obsessed with firearms and Dance Dance Revolution, woke up one morning, murdered his mother, and then proceeded to the local elementary school where, in a span of five minutes, he systematically executed twenty small children and several adults, and then shot himself in the head. Why would someone do such a terrible thing? There's never a satisfying answer to that question. In the aftermath, Alex Jones, a sleazy YouTube conspiracy theorist, somehow managed to convince large segments of his viewership that this stomach-turning atrocity was staged by paid actors, encouraging his followers to harass the grieving parents. Why would someone do such a terrible thing? Well, in Jones' case, the motivation was clear: to generate thousands of viewer subscriptions and sell a lot of dodgy nutritional supplements. Apparently, the enterprise has been quite profitable—Jones was recently sued by the Sandy Hook parents for nearly a billion dollars. (He plans, of course, to appeal.)

Or consider the case of Ron DeSantis, the Republican governor of Florida, who recently amused himself by shipping busloads of desperate asylum-seekers—from Texas—to the wealthy liberal enclave of Martha's Vineyard, with all the moral consideration of a teenager ordering a pizza for the neighbors as a prank. Why? Because sometimes—as Adam Serwer of *The Atlantic* put it—the cruelty *is* the point.

As the human race has grown into a single global network, deep-rooted irrationality, greed, and cussed human nature are now writ large, encoded into vast systemic structures that threaten the very survival of our species. "Whatever happened to digging the well for the man who comes after?" wonders Robert Vicaray, the founding member of the Rude Mechanicals. A radical environmentalist who grew up in a known cancer-belt and helplessly watched his mother sicken and die, he has begun to suspect that he is "living through the commission of a new form of genocide." For decades, politicians and industry lobbyists have ridiculed the dire warnings of climate scientists; now that profound environmental changes have become self-evident to all but a stubborn few, the nay-sayers have switched tactics. They'll admit, begrudgingly, that some unusual and unpleasant climate events *might* be occurring, but simultaneously insist that human activity has played no role in causing them, and should therefore play no role in preventing or addressing them. Business must go on as usual, regardless of the existential stakes. Meanwhile, California and Colorado are burning, and hurricanes strike the eastern seaboard with increasing frequency and strength, most recently Hurricane Ian, the fifth worst storm to hit the United States in recorded history. Lives lost, homes destroyed, communities devastated, families displaced. As Kurt Vonnegut would say: So it goes.

Acts of God, Acts of Man. The distinction is a crucial one to Oscar Louder, the insurance adjuster who, out of a kind of moral exhaustion, eventually throws in his lot in with the Rude Mechanics. "Active God," muses a desperate claimant who has lost his business in a disaster. "Didn't know the insurance companies had religion." But what the man really wants to know, with great urgency, is how he's going to pay his overdue loans and keep food on his family's table. In an instructive passage, Oscar methodically explains how insurance policies work in natural disasters, how insurance companies and government agencies, guided by rational self-interest, do their utmost to refuse or delay claims, and how this frustrating process can be further stymied by legislation in those states—such as Florida—that forbid individual claimants from directly negotiating with Federal agencies such as FEMA, forcing disaster victims to rely on the intermediary of their own recalcitrant, self-interested insurance companies.

Acts of God are compounded by Acts of Man. In Oscar's travels with the Rude Mechanicals, he witnesses the human costs firsthand and increasingly finds the distinction between God and Man blurred. *"Cui bono?"* he is fond of muttering to himself. Large, impersonal organizations somehow always manage to reap a profit from human misery.

We are, of course, just emerging—or so we hope—from a spectacularly notable global disaster, accompanied by an unprecedented tidal wave of death and misery, and, alas, by a proportionate measure of cruelty, stupidity, malfeasance, and profiteering. It is not all surprising to learn from the Author's Note—which you should definitely read—that much of this novel was composed during the height of the pandemic while the author was sequestered under lockdown at his home in Seville.

A smoldering moral outrage burns through *Blue Rhinoceros*. As one of the two first-person narrators—we'll get to the second momentarily—Thomas Entrecarceles, the disgraced journalist, is a well-chosen vehicle for the fury: articulate, erudite, and deeply familiar with the evil ways of the world. When we first meet him, he is a ruined man, shunned by his former colleagues and friends, scorned by the public, and brutally betrayed by someone he loved. Indeed, he has been quite soberly considering suicide when Sairy walks through his door. It's hard to say why Sairy's case, bizarre though it is, intrigues him enough to put his plans to end his life on hold. Thomas seems indifferent to the great sum of money Sairy offers him to investigate her past; this is a stop-gap, at best, and no amount of money will restore his former life. Curiosity, perhaps, at least initially. It's as good a reason as any to keep on living. Or perhaps the case offers Thomas one last chance to practice his former vocation, to painstakingly excavate the scattered shards of a long-forgotten story and piece them back together. But there's something deeper, murkier, at work here, some dark and unresolved metaphysical suspicion troubling his soul.

The case takes over Thomas's life, and he is often driven to extraordinary lengths in his quest to reconstruct the circumstances surrounding Sairy and the blue rhinoceros. The disaster that struck Littoral seventeen years ago was spectacularly newsworthy, and yet it has been largely forgotten by the world. The living witnesses Thomas tracks down don't want to talk about that terrible day, or the terrible things that happened in its aftermath. Why? Grief, shame, and complicity all play a role, but as the scope of the investigation expands, Thomas begins to attract the attention of more sinister entities who would prefer that this particular skeleton stays buried. His life is threatened more than once. Thomas remains undeterred, determined to find his way to the center of the web, until he begins to discern the shape of something so unthinkable that even he recoils in disbelief.

In Thomas's private narrative, we are presented with the reconstructed events of 2012 as they happen, often from the intimate viewpoints of the characters who experienced them. But research on a long-cold case like this can only take you so far. Another narrator—one with far greater powers of omniscience—steps in to fill in the gaps: the author himself. In the Author's Note to *Blue Rhinoceros* (I told you to read it) Salvo warns us that he plans to intrude, but insists that he is "an altogether different person, with different opinions and a different disposition, from the wretchedly jaded Thomas Entrecarceles," who is "very much his own person." To help us distinguish between the two, Salvo will identify himself "as '*this writer*' as opposed to Mr. Entrecarceles' favored '*this journalist*'."

To this reader, that predetermined scheme seems to be something of an elaborate ruse. Entrecarceles' voice, style, and, indeed, opinions and disposition, are generally indistinguishable from Salvo's. If those identifying tags ("journalist," "writer") were deployed to indicate which narrator was on deck, I failed to take notice, generally too engrossed in the story to care. Whether reconstructed or decanted straight from the source, the events of 2012 are recounted from an omniscient point-of-view, dipping into individual characters' thoughts, feelings, and private doings at will, often providing us with relevant information that the characters themselves are not privy to. Both narrators have an engaging, world-weary style, but an oddly formal one that feels more rooted in the mid-twentieth century than the mid-twenty-first. Perhaps this is the influence of Joseph Mitchell, who is invoked in that Author's Note, in a long tongue-in-cheek list of authors whom Salvo claims to have plagiarized. (Several works by Kurt Vonnegut are also listed, but while Vonnegut's literary DNA is readily discernible in the topsy-turvy, brutal universe of *Blue Rhinoceros*, he does not seem to have been a major influence on Salvo's writing style.)

Both narrators have similar faults, too. Whether writing as Entrecarceles or as himself, Salvo often indulges a writerly pleasure in his own flights of rhetoric. He is fond of turning a fine phrase—perhaps a little too fond, at times—and prone to pontificating, especially when waxing philosophical about ethical matters and the underlying motivations and circumstances that lead people to do terrible things. But to be fair, we were forewarned about this sermonizing tendency in Salvo's introduction, and if this is a flaw, it is a Melvillian one, a fundamental characteristic of the novel that would be difficult to excise without diminishing the greatness of the whole. And Salvo has a mellifluous voice, so it's easy to forgive him for occasionally taking one too many solos.

What does allow us to identify which narrator we are dealing with is that both Salvo and Entrecarceles are characters in themselves, so we are clued in when, for example, Thomas mentions an interview or encounter taking place in the present time, or when Salvo breaks the fourth wall by (for example) disclosing why he, the author, has assigned certain fates to certain charac-

ters. But because their voices are so similar, it often takes us a while to figure out who is in the driver's seat. A kind of uncentered, stereoscopic effect emerges from this narrative approach, an effect entirely appropriate to a story which is already unsettled by design, where all versions of events are provisional, fragmented, prone to revision and tainted by falsehood, shifting under our feet like a Florida sinkhole. This is, after all, a novel willing to take on the unsettling question: *Why would someone kill the last living blue rhinoceros? Why would someone do such a terrible thing?* Maybe, as Bruce Springsteen put it, there's just a meanness in this world. But I suspect that Oscar Louder, the exacting insurance adjuster, would answer this question with a question: *Cui bono?*

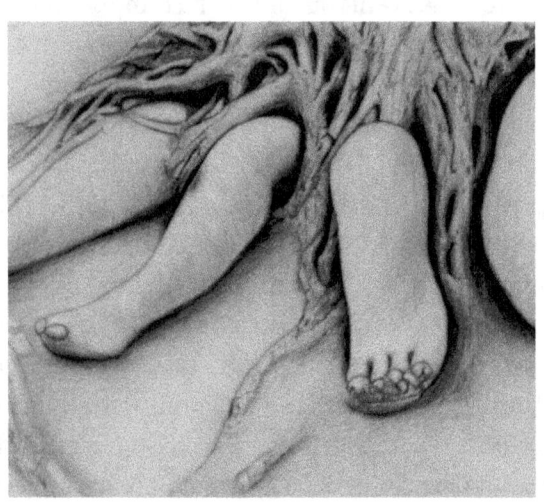

CHRISTOPHER BOUCHER

THE WORD PARTY

That weekend, a few words and phrases held a party to celebrate the completion of *Exacting Clam 7*—the phrase "Executive Homes" sent out an email inviting all of the issue's editors, contributors, and words. I wasn't going to go, but then a sentence I knew from the issue, "Authors don't own

their texts, not once they hand it over to us," texted me to check in. *Hey man you going?* wrote the sentence. *Should be 'potentially infinite'!*

Nah, think I'm gonna pass, I wrote back.

Boo!, wrote "Authors." *"Devil-may-care's" going! And "like an ocean!"*

Any other writers? I replied. *Or just language?*

No I think a few writers too—Luchs? maybe Silverton??

So I decided to go. My father had died the previous winter, and the months since had been the loneliest of my life. I couldn't remember the last time I'd been invited to a party. This would be good for me, I thought.

But when I stepped out of the Uber that Friday night and walked into the fancy home, I didn't see one other person; it was all words and phrases—hardly any of whom I recognized. I saw "the five allottable shrugs," sitting in a leather chair in the giant living room and sipping what looked like whiskey, and I ran into "reluctant false messiah" in the kitchen near an elaborate spread of hors d'oeuvres. "Dude!" said "reluctant." "Quite a crib, huh?"

"Whose place is this?" I said.

"Reluctant" shook his head. "I think 'Executive Homes' is renting it."

I poured myself a glass of punch—it was very strong—and walked out into the backyard. "Your efficient facility for apology" shouted my name from behind the grill, and I saw a few other words swimming in the pool and milling near the dance floor. Then I spotted "Authors don't own their texts, not once they hand it over to us," making out with "What matters are our feelings, our responses, what it means when it passes through the filter of us" in a corner, and "just the title alone" passed out on a nearby chaise lounge. A lot of the language appeared to be drunk.

I sat down with my punch by the pool's edge. A word cannonballed off the diving board. I stared into the turquoise water, and then out at the woods at the edge of the yard. This was quite an expanse.

I hadn't been sitting there a minute, though, when "cyclonic culture" sat down beside me. "Chris!" he said. "Hey man!"

I nodded at him.

"Great jam, huh?" he said.

Behind us, digital music began blasting through the speakers.

"'Cyclonic,'" I said quietly. "I'm the only writer here."

"So what?" The phrase twisted around and looked behind us, where some words had started dancing. "Hey," he said. "Wanna dance? Let's dance."

"I want to *leave*," I said.

"You just got here!" said "cyclonic culture." "Come on. Don't be a *writer*. Let's cut a rug!" He got up and I reluctantly followed. "Executive" had set up a temporary dance floor on the lawn, and a few phrases I knew—"devil-may-care," "mellifluous laughter," "continually mingling and separating"—were vibing to the music. I tried to follow suit—to loosen up and find the groove. I was making my best effort to have fun, be social, and enjoy the night. One song morphed into another, and more phrases seeped onto the floor. My mind and belly warmed from the punch. We were all celebrating something. I closed my eyes and bounced to the beat. I felt, for the first time in a while, happy.

But then, suddenly, someone shouted from off to my right—"Hey! It's him!" or something like that. I opened my eyes and saw a phrase I barely knew, "My previous friend," holding a bottle of beer in one letter and pointing at me with another. "That's the guy!" he bellowed at "The gauntlet has definitely been thrown." "That's the guy who wrote the story."

"What story?" shouted "gauntlet."

"*The* story, man!" spat "my previous friend." "The word party one! The one with *you* and *me* in it." "Friend" turned to me. "You're Bowcher, right?"

"I—yeah," I said meekly.

"Yeah! You're the asshole who put all of us in your story. Without even *asking* us!"

"He what?" said a phrase behind me.

"Easy, man," "continually mingling and separating" said to "my previous friend." "It's alright—it's OK."

"It is *not* OK," said "my previous friend," now vibrating with rage. "You wrote about me, and 'gauntlet,' and 'like an ocean,' and—"

"Wait," said "like an ocean." "You wrote about *me*?"

"Just let me explain," I said.

"You had no right," barked "friend." "No *right!*"

"I—listen," I yelled, trying to be heard over the music. "I just thought it'd be fun to write a story that, you know, included other writing from the same issue—"

"Fun!" yelped "my previous friend." He smashed his bottle on the dance floor. "You thought it'd be *fun?*" Then he lunged at me.

"Whoa!" shouted "cyclonic culture." "Take it easy!"

"Yeah, 'friend'—back off!" boomed "reluctant false messiah," and he shoved "my previous friend" backwards.

"*You* fucking back off!" shouted "gauntlet," reaching for "messiah."

Someone threw a punch. "Friend" dove at "messiah," and "ocean" headbutted "cyclonic." All the phrases started shouting and fighting, and soon it was a melee; I saw "gauntlet" on the ground, and "continually mingling and separating" bleeding from his "c," and "devil-may-care" doubled over. I covered my head and struggled out of the scrum. I heard a window break, and then someone pushed the grill into the pool. I stared dumbly at the chaos for a second, trying to decide what to do.

But then I heard a whining in the distance—we all heard it. "Cops!" shouted "a corny geometry to endings." Everyone ran. "Corny" steered me and some other phrases away from the house. "This way!" he said, and he led us into the dark woods.

"This is so fucked up!" shouted "mellifluous laughter."

"Where are we going?" I cried.

"There's a gulley somewhere ahead," whispered "Our minds wander."

"But I can't *see!*" shouted a word I couldn't read.

"We *cannot* fucking get arrested," said "the five allottable shrugs." "That'll totally derail the issue!"

We ran deeper into the woods. "A corny geometry to endings" was near me for a while, along with "drunk and walking alone to that cold home" and "you are alone and it is over." But I lost "endings" somewhere, and then "drunk and walking alone." Then it was just me and "you are alone and it is over." But when I said, "Look! A clearing!" and heard no response, I realized that I'd lost "you," too. I sprinted onto the asphalt of a strange street and ran on alone through the cold, silent night.

Contributors

Jacob M. Appel is the author of many novels and short story collections including *The Man Who Wouldn't Stand Up*, *Scouting for the Reaper*, *Phoning Home*, *Einstein's Beach House*, and *Millard Salter's Last Day*. His short fiction has appeared in many literary journals including *Agni, Colorado Review, Gettysburg Review*, and more. His essays have appeared in *The New York Times, Chicago Tribune, Detroit Free Press, Orlando Sentinel, The Providence Journal*, and many regional newspapers. He has taught most recently at Brown University, at the Gotham Writers' Workshop in New York City, and at Yeshiva College, where he was the writer-in-residence.

Corina Bardoff is a writer and librarian currently living in New Jersey. Her fiction has appeared in *Storm Cellar, Menacing Hedge, Hysterical, Cream City Review*, and elsewhere.

Christopher Bernard is the author of *A Spy in the Ruins* and many other books. He wrote: "I believe in redemption, if any, through the delicacy of fantasy, the reverie that vanishes in its realization, vertigo of the moment's adoration, the convivial grace of the hallucinations called art."

Tori Bond is the author of *Familyism* (Matter Press 2019), a collection of flash fiction. Her work has appeared in *McSweeney's Internet Tendency, Monkeybicycle, Atticus Review, Flash Fiction Funny* anthology, and others. She holds an MFA in Creative Writing from Rosemont College and studied comedy writing at The Second City.

Kevin Boniface, an artist, writer and postman in Huddersfield, West Yorkshire, UK, is the author of *Round About Town* (Uniformbooks, 2018) and *Lost in the Post* (Old Street Publishing, 2008).

Christopher Boucher is the author of the novels *How to Keep Your Volkswagen Alive* (Melville House, 201), *Golden Delicious* (MH, 2016), and *Big Giant Floating Head* (MH, 2019). He teaches writing and literature at Boston College and is Managing Editor of *Post Road Magazine*.

Ian Boulton is a writer and editor living at the English seaside, having returned home after spells working abroad in Ukraine, Mongolia, Russia and Turkmenistan. He has published about twenty short stories in various outlets over the past eleven years. Last year he contributed to Dodo Ink's *Trauma* collection.

Steven Breyak is an American poet who lives with his wife and son in Osaka, Japan, where he teaches English.

Marvin Cohen is the author of many novels, plays, and collections of essays, stories, and poems. He lives on the Lower East Side of Manhattan.

Alec Demitrus is a traveler, writer, and board-game fanatic. When not exploring the world and nature, he can be found in Denver with a book or beer in his hand.

Jack Foley's numerous books of poetry, fiction and criticism include *Visions and Affiliations*, a "chronoencyclopedia" of California poetry from 1940 to 2005, *Grief Songs* (SM, 2017) and *When Sleep Comes* (SM, 2020). He lives in Oakland and hosts a weekly radio show, *Cover to Cover*, on Berkeley's Pacifica station, KPFA.

Jake Goldsmith is a writer with cystic fibrosis and the founder of The Barbellion Prize, a book prize for ill and disabled authors. He is the author of a memoir, *Neither Weak Nor Obtuse* (SM, 2022).

Tyler C. Gore's essays, stories, and reviews have appeared in many of the fine, high-quality journals preferred by discerning readers like you. He is the author of *My Life of Crime: Essays and Other Entertainments* (Sagging Meniscus, 2022), a delightful book that you should definitely buy. He lives, as he dreams—in Brooklyn.

John Patrick Higgins is a playwright, short story writer, screenwriter and director. He lives in Belfast.

Nick Holdstock is the author of two novels, *The Casualties* and *Quarantine*, and a short story collection, *The False River*.

Kurt Luchs is the author of *Falling in the Direction of Up* (SM, 2020), *One of These Things Is Not Like the Other* (Finishing Line Press, 2019), and the humor collection *It's Funny Until Someone Loses an Eye (Then It's Really Funny)* (SM, 2017). He lives in Michigan.

Melissa McCarthy's *Sharks, Death, Surfers: An Illustrated Companion* was published by Sternberg in

2019. Her next book, *Photo, Phyto, Proto, Nitro*, comes out with Sagging Meniscus in the autumn of 2023. In the meantime, other pieces from *Full Stop* magazine, *Public Domain Review*, *The Yellow Paper*, and more; and her two radio series—Melissa McCarthy's *View from a Shark* and *The Slipping Forecast*—can be found at sharksillustrated.org. She lives in Edinburgh.

Jim Meirose's work has appeared in numerous venues. His novels include *Sunday Dinner with Father Dwyer* (Optional Books), *Understanding Franklin Thompson* (JEF), *Le Overgivers au Club de la Résurrection* (Mannequin Haus), and *No and Maybe—Maybe and No* (Pski's Porch).

Kathleen Nicholls is an author and illustrator, best known for *Go Your Crohn Way*, the first of three books loosely based on her own experiences with chronic illness. She lives and works in central Scotland.

M.J. Nicholls is the author of the novels *Trimming England* (SM, 2021), *Scotland Before the Bomb* (SM, 2019), The *1002nd Book to Read Before You Die* (SM, 2018), *The Quiddity of Delusion* (SM, 2017), *The House of Writers* (SM, 2016), and *A Postmodern Belch* (2014). He lives in Glasgow.

Paolo Pergola is the author of *Passaggi—avventure di un autostoppista* (Rides: The Adventures of a Hitchhiker) (Exorma, 2013), *Attraverso la finestra di Snell* (Through Snell's Window) (Italo Svevo Edizione, 2019), and *Reset* (SM, 2021). His work has appeared in several Italian literary magazines. He is a member of OPLEPO/Opificio di Letteratura Potenziale (Workshop of Potential Literature), Italy's equivalent of France's OULIPO. He lives in Tuscany and works as a zoologist.

Randy Prunty lives in the Bay Area where he works as a bus driver. You can see some of his recent work in *New American Writing*, *Fence*, *Parentheses* and upcoming in *Volt* and *Poemeleon*. His latest chapbook is *Pretend I'm Me*, out from the micropress Ethel.

Jesse Salvo is a native New Yorker but now lives in Seville, Spain. His work has been published in over a dozen literary journals including *Hobart Pulp*, *Maudlin House*, *Barren Magazine*, *Menacing Hedge*, *X-Ray Lit*, others. Before that, he spent three years working for online comedy magazines. His first novel, *Blue Rhinoceros*, debuted in May 2022 courtesy of New Meridian Arts. Salvo serves as senior fiction editor and contributing columnist for *Bull Magazine*.

Mike Silverton's poetry appeared in the late 60s and early 70s in *Harper's*, *The Nation*, *Wormwood Review*, *Poetry Now*, *some/thing*, *Chelsea*, *Prairie Schooner*, *Elephant* and elsewhere. William Cole included Mike's poems in four anthologies: *Eight Lines and Under* (Macmillan, 1967), *Pith and Vinegar* (Simon and Schuster, 1969), *Poetry Brief* (Macmillan, 1971), and *Poems One Line & Longer* (Grossman, 1973).

Walter Smart, a Senior Fellow of the Institute of Krinst Studies, is suspicious of corn. He edited J.F. Mamjjasond and Fafnir Finkelmeyer's *Hoptime* for Sagging Meniscus (2016).

Paul Stanbridge is the author of *Forbidden Line* (Galley Beggar, 2016) and *My Mind to Me a Kingdom Is* (Galley Beggar, 2022).

Terese Svoboda is the author of 20 books. She has won the Bobst Prize in fiction, the Iowa Prize for poetry, an NEH grant for translation, the Graywolf Nonfiction Prize, a Jerome Foundation prize for video, the O. Henry award for the short story, and a Pushcart Prize for the essay. She is a three time winner of the New York Foundation for the Arts fellowship, and has been awarded Headlands, James Merrill, Hawthornden, Hermitage, Yaddo, McDowell, and Bellagio residencies. Her opera WET premiered at L.A.'s Disney Hall.

Eileen R. Tabios has released over 60 collections of poetry, fiction, essays, and experimental biographies.

Rodrigo Toscano is a poet and essayist based in New Orleans. He is the author of ten books of poetry. His latest book is *The Charm & The Dread* (Fence Books, 2021). His *Collapsible Poetics Theater* was a National Poetry Series selection. His poetry has appeared in *Best American Poetry* and *Best American Experimental Poetry*.

Thomas Walton is the author of *Good Morning Bone Crusher!* (Spuyten Duyvil, 2021), *All the Useless Things Are Mine* (Sagging Meniscus, 2020), *The World Is All That Does Befall Us* (Ravenna Press, 2019), and *The Last Mosaic* with Elizabeth Cooperman, Sagging Meniscus, 2018). His work has appeared in *ZYZZYVA*, *Delmar*, *Timberline Review*, *Rivet*, *Stringtown Magazine*, *Queen Mob's Teahouse*, *Bombay Gin*, *Pontoon*, and other magazines. He lives in Seattle, WA.

www.ingramcontent.com/pod-product-compliance
Lightning Source LLC
Chambersburg PA
CBHW080820250626
47159CB00011B/3451